ECHOES OF TYRANNY

FREEDOM LOST

PART II OF THE FACTORY SAGA

WRITTEN BY
ANTONIO MELONIO

To the dreamers.

PROLOGUE

Three figures, silhouettes in the twilight, trudged across a grassy plain toward a forest of twisted metal and broken concrete. For weeks, they had walked south from the valley – over mountains, through endless forests, and across weary flatlands. Sunburn and the winds of spring had carved tributes to exhaustion into their faces. Each step ushered in pain, yet they pressed on, pulled by some silent urgency.

They had finally arrived.

Eyes alert, they scanned the horizon for movement, half-expecting the nightmares of their past to reawaken. When nothing stirred but wilted grass and glassy rubble shimmering in the dying light, Wilder raised a hand to halt them. Ahead lay devastation. It was blackness and despair. A sharp border separated grass from ruin, life from death. An unnatural duality, like the creatures that had transformed these travelers – once hunters – into the hunted.

Wilder produced a lantern and lit it with practiced hands. Its small flame caught the length of his long hair, illuminating a smile that wavered between excitement and caution. He gestured forward, and the three of them crossed that stark boundary, leaving the world behind for the dark wasteland.

What a glorious place this must have been, Wilder thought, as they climbed the wreckage. He imagined the clamor of machinery, the order and purpose of a booming industry, that endless tower his grandfather had spoken of. A golden crown now gone molten, turned to dust, swallowed by decades. A shiver of regret traced his spine. We made a terrible mistake. Only destruction and chaos remained where once there had been hierarchy and purpose – a world in which everyone had known their place.

"Keep your eyes peeled for anything useful," said Wilder. The debris groaned beneath their steps. The air reeked of rust and rot, the metal still radiating the sun's warmth. "And be careful."

Heather and Brook nodded, following a few paces behind. They had lost two scouts over the winter, sent out but never returned, leaving no signs, no remains – nothing. Families back in the valley had begun to ask questions – questions Wilder answered with half-truths and distractions. No one could find out what they were really doing, or their dream would die in the womb. Someday, he thought, they would understand.

One scout, however, did return. Wolf, the beast of a man, had returned raving about horrors that made no sense. Wilder hadn't believed him at first. He'd been angry at Wolf's refusal to go out again. Now, Wilder knew better. Terror had become his nightly companion. Still, Wolf's stories – and his map – had been worth the price. The man had seen and understood.

A noise broke the silence. A chunk of concrete crashed to the ground.

"Did you hear that?" Heather asked, pausing. She brushed silver, sweat-slicked hair from her forehead. It stuck to her temples.

"No," Brook whispered, turning. "What do –"

A shriek erupted across the dead landscape, slicing the air with raw anguish. Wilder's lantern quivered, and they all froze, eyes wide with fear. The cry sounded like torture incarnate – pain, despair, and some faint longing. I know that longing, Wilder thought. I feel it, too.

"Quiet," Wilder said. He swept hair from his face and pulled up his sleeves, revealing the eagle tattoo coiled around his forearm like it might spring to life. The shriek faded. The world went still.

Brook eyed Wilder, remembering the first time he'd seen that same wild look in his friend's eyes: they'd been children then, when Wilder had forced another boy to kill a stray dog. Brook still remembered the dog's whimper, the rock rising and falling, the tears. Wilder's fascinated gaze. His cold grin. They'd done worse things since. But soon, all of it would be worth it. The valley, their people – they'd be safe once this was over. Brook clung to that hope even as the memory pried at the cracks in his mind.

Suddenly, another shriek, from a new direction.

"Was that...?" Brook's voice wavered. A trembling hand crept to the dagger at his belt.

"It's still far away," Wilder murmured. "Move in silence." He glanced at Brook – on the brink of panic. The man's breaths came shallow and frantic, his body tensed to run. He won't get far if he tries, Wilder thought.

"You can do this," Heather said, squeezing her husband's hand, her voice low but steady. "Breathe."

Brook forced air into his lungs. The pounding in his chest finally slowed.

"Remember why we're here," Wilder said, putting his hands on Brook's shoulders. The man was in need of reassurance. They had grown up together, endured countless hardships. When Wilder's wife had died, Brook had been the first person he'd told about his dream: an eagle soaring to a golden throne, the restoration of civilization, a future forged in order. "Brook, brother. Come on." His voice cut through the treacherous silence. "Let's find that chamber and get the hell out of here."

Brook mustered a nod, slapped his face to refocus, rubbed his balding head, and pulled himself together. Heather kissed him, slapped his ass, and they advanced anew, hearts hammering with that primal knowledge of prey sensing its predator in the shadows. No escape routes left, nothing left to do but fight and wage bloody war. Survive another day.

For hours, they navigated rubble, jumped twisted beams, scaled collapsed walls. All the while, the creature's shrieks circled closer, nearer – hunting them as they hunted beasts in the valley. Flanking, watching, waiting. By the time the screams became a constant drone, their nerves were frayed beyond measure.

"I don't like this," Brook muttered through clenched teeth. "I don't like this at all."

"Just keep moving," Wilder growled. He focused on his lantern's comforting light. He had been the predator before. He knew all too well the chilling moment when prey realized it had lost. Sweat poured down his temples, but he pressed on, occasionally checking the knife at his belt.

Another shriek ripped the stale air. Very close now.

"We're almost there," Wilder whispered.

Brook sucked in air and stared ahead. "How the fuck did Wolf make it alone?"

"The man's a beast," said Wilder.

Within moments, shrieks piled on shrieks. A maddening wail that drilled into their minds, relentless and deafening. They abandoned caution and broke into a sprint, heads spinning with migraine-like agony. Just when it felt like the creature had cornered them, Heather spotted a black door hidden in the wreckage. She quickly confirmed the door was the one on Wolf's map.

"There!" She shoved Brook forward. "Go!"

Behind them came the sound of furious strides. It was faster than they had imagined – closing in with terrifying speed. The trio dove into the debris, their arms and legs scraping on jagged shards of metal. They tumbled toward the open door and shoved it shut just as the creature slammed against it. A shock wave reverberated through the door, jarring their arms and shoulders, threatening to snap bone from socket.

"Hold on!" Wilder yelled.

They braced themselves against the metal barrier, heartbeats thundering in their ears. Through a momentary gap, they glimpsed pale limbs spattered with dried blood, a misshapen torso loping on all fours, its face contorted by pain and rage. They slammed the door again, muscles burning, as the creature crashed into the barrier over and over, shrieking so loud it felt like nails scraping across their skulls. At last, the onslaught diminished into nothing. Its steps retreated. But still they stood pressed against the door, unwilling to trust that silence.

"You think it's gone?" Heather's voice trembled. Her legs were shaking.

"I don't know," Wilder said, exhaling. "But we can't stay here." He wiped sweat from his brow and stepped back. "It might be finding another way in."

They paused, waiting for the worst. Still breathing? Good enough. Brook and Heather peeled themselves from the door. Then they turned toward the room behind them. And when Wilder's lantern swept the darkness, hope filled the stale air.

"This is it," Wilder said, his voice quivering with triumph. "We found it."

Rats scurried in the corners, scattering from the glow. A battered desk stood near the far wall, lit-

tered with ancient papers and a shattered tablet –
like the ones Ren, that smug suit, sometimes carried. But that wasn't what seized their attention.

Heather and Brook exchanged a look of wonder.
Dusty racks lined the walls. Most were empty, but
some bore the dark outlines of metal and wood.
Wolf had found the black door, but not this, Wilder
remembered. Only they had made it this far, the
first to enter since the revolution buried this place.

"So these are rifles?" Brook asked, gingerly lifting
one of the ancient contraptions. His fear evaporated
for a moment, replaced by curiosity.

"How do you –"

"Careful," Wilder warned, pointing one rifle toward the door with a grin that made him look
younger. "These are no toys."

He explained what his grandfather had taught
him: how to load, how to kill. Words were one
thing, the reality another. There would be time to
train in the depths of the forests back home, away
from the valley's prying eyes. For now, they'd learn
by doing.

A fresh shriek thundered from above. Dust rained down, and a terrible scraping noise – something was burrowing through the debris. Metal moaned as it shifted.

They froze. This shriek sounded different. Deeper. Another creature. One above, one somewhere by the door. Scuffling footsteps told them the first beast had returned.

"No time!" Wilder shouted, tossing boxes of ammunition to Heather and Brook. "Load up like I showed you!" His grin was feverish with pride. They had come here to restore order, to resurrect a broken dream. "Let's take control. No more fear! No more weakness!" This was what he lived for. Pure, unaltered experience.

Just then, the first creature lunged into the open doorway. Wilder clenched his jaw and squeezed the trigger. The rifle roared. The beast's head exploded in a spray of gore. Recoil jolted Wilder's shoulder, his ears ringing. Heather and Brook stared, stunned by the sheer power of it.

Wilder laughed into the smoke and chaos, pain radiating from his shoulder. The scraping above stopped. Lantern in hand, he bolted out the door, refusing to let the second creature escape. He was God now – dealing death at the pull of a trigger. No longer prey. Never again the victim.

He remembered his wife, lying feverish in her final hours. If the old days had survived, Wilder had often thought, they'd have had medicine for her. He would rebuild that golden empire. He would restore the Factory. Spying the larger creature mid-leap across a wrecked beam, Wilder steadied his aim, grinning. This is for you. He fired, and the crumbling wasteland reverberated with the thunderous echo of annihilation.

The Factory was alive. It had merely slept.

SUMMER: CHAPTER 1

The sun had barely cleared the treetops when Ava, Hazel, and Janis descended the forest slope, their teenage laughter rippling through the morning haze. As they rounded a bend, the river opened up before them – a silver ribbon reflecting sky and branches alike. A sweet floral perfume mingled with the earthy scent of moss and damp wood. Somewhere overhead, songbirds trilled a welcome to the day.

Janis dashed ahead, his footsteps scattering pine needles. "Guys! There it is! Hurry up!"

He ditched his shoes by the riverbank and plopped down on a flat boulder, letting the frigid water numb his ankles. Ava and Hazel followed suit, settling onto nearby stones. With a self-important flourish, Janis brandished his fishing rod.

"Listen carefully," he said. "You want the bait snug on the hook, like this." He fidgeted, dropping a worm once or twice. "Yeah, well... something like that."

Hazel, who had never fished before, asked a barrage of questions about worms and bites and how they'd know if a fish was on the line. She seemed especially concerned that worms might feel pain. Janis claimed his mother had assured him they didn't. Worms didn't have nerve endings or something. Hazel still looked skeptical, but half the fun for her was listening to Janis ramble. Ava, on the other hand, had no trouble casting her line. She flicked it out into the current with easy grace.

"Of course, we might be here all day without a single nibble," Janis muttered, scratching his head. "There used to be a lot more fish, Mom says. Now –"

Ava's startled cry broke his sentence. Her rod bowed sharply, line tearing circles in the water.

"Don't let go!" Janis cried, stumbling over himself as he rushed to help. Hazel hurried behind him.

"Thanks," Ava gasped. "I was obviously planning on dropping it. Thought that might be a good idea."

The three of them wrestled the rod until at last Ava hauled in a writhing trout, glimmering in the morning sun. She slammed it against a rock until it went limp – Hazel turned away, grimacing. The trout's belly was covered in odd red lesions. Janis insisted it wasn't dangerous, just some reaction to the warming water. None of them seemed particularly convinced.

"Holy crap, Ava, you're a natural!" Hazel exclaimed once she'd recovered her composure.

Ava shrugged, looking equally surprised. "Dad taught me a while back."

"Yeah... great job," Janis managed, trying not to sound too wounded in his pride. "But it's, uh... not that big."

Ava smirked. "Big enough."

They kept fishing – without much success – for another hour, passing around lukewarm cider from Janis's pack. A family of ducks bobbed nearby, and a small herd of deer browsed on the far side of the bank. Noon arrived, hot and relentless; soon, sweat beaded on their foreheads as the conversation meandered between idle gossip and aimless wondering.

"You ever think about what's beyond those mountains?" Janis asked, nodding toward the towering, snow-capped ridges at the horizon. The river they sat beside was born somewhere in those heights, plunging underground and reemerging who-knew-where.

"Maybe it's a whole new world waiting to be discovered!" Hazel's blue eyes glinted with the fervor of cider. She leaped to her feet, wobbling. "We could just go. Be explorers! Escape this boring valley and actually live our lives for once!"

Janis liked how her hair swung around her shoulders, how excitement sparked in her face. He forced himself to look away. "I'll stick around," he said softly. He pictured his sick mother back home – her best days weren't really good anymore, and on her worst days, she barely spoke. The whole community helped, of course, but he couldn't just abandon her. "Anyway, adventurous types end up lonely. I like having people around."

"I hear you," Ava agreed. "Dad always warned me it's nothing but danger in those mountains. Starving wolves, disease-carrying mosquitoes... you name it."

Hazel sipped from her mug, unruffled by Ava's caution. She watched the ducks floating on the water's surface, envy biting at her. What a life – no heartbreak, no overthinking, no dreaded confessions. Just paddle and bob, up and down, forever, until the end.

Janis traced a fingertip through the current. "There has to be something else out there, though. Other communities. Other people."

Hazel's lips curled into a half smile. "Yeah, it's nice to wonder about all kinds of things, right? All kinds of... people." She blushed when the words slipped out, hoping no one noticed. Her mouth had run away from her, fueled by too much cider.

Janis's grin turned sly. "Oh, Hazel. Something you're not telling us?" He bumped her playfully with his elbow, bushy eyebrows dancing. His heart sank just a bit when he saw how red Hazel's cheeks got.

"Of course not!" Hazel insisted. Her voice wavered. "I tell you guys everything."

Ava's eyes lit with teasing. "Aha, so there is a new crush."

Hazel's face burned a deeper shade of crimson. "What? No crush. None."

Janis perched forward. "Come on, it's obvious." Please be me, he thought. Just this once.

"It's Aspen, isn't it?" Ava said, gazing into Hazel's wide blue eyes.

Hazel swallowed thickly. "No – no, that's ridic –"

"I knew it!" Ava let out a triumphant laugh.

Hazel slumped, arms folded. "He only showed up last week to help with our apple trees," she muttered. "We barely talked, okay?"

"Damn, it really is Aspen," said Janis, feeling his already fragile masculinity take another hit. "I hate that guy. Perfect face. Perfect hair. Taller every time I see him. I'll be single forever." He flung a rock into the river, narrowly missing a duck.

"Aw, Janis." Ava patted him sympathetically.

He ignored her, launching into a tirade about Aspen's dancing at the solstice festival – six partners in one night. Six! Meanwhile, Janis had been stuck with old Mossbeard's depressing monologues about the Factory. Ava teased him about the drunken warbling that had followed, when Janis and Mossbeard had proudly, and very loudly, sung 'Pascal of the Revolution', that old revolutionary hymn. Even Janis found himself laughing.

"Anyway," Janis said, once he'd caught his breath, "let's discuss the future Mr. and Mrs. Aspen over here." He forced a playful smirk, ignoring the twinge in his chest. "You two will settle down, fill the valley with your tall, charming brood –"

"Excuse me," Hazel objected, cheeks flushing again. "They'd be wise and pretty, too, thank you very much."

"And smart like moose," he retorted.

Ava snorted. "Moose aren't particularly smart, are they?"

They all dissolved into laughter, cider sloshing in their cups.

When talk inevitably circled back to Aspen, Ava mentioned rumors about his parents – they'd been gone for weeks, maybe months, leaving Aspen alone in that sprawling house. Such a disappearance wasn't uncommon for them, but still...

Hazel's blush deepened even further. "Why did no one tell me?" she asked, voice shaking with a mix of concern and embarrassment. Poor Aspen. All alone in that big house and no one to keep him company.

Janis set his cup aside. "Apparently, his parents tried to recruit my mom for something."

"Recruit her?" Ava's brow furrowed. "For what?"

"No clue. She got mad when I asked. Said they were 'poisoning the community' and she wanted to bring it up at the next assembly." He paused, swirling the dregs in his cup. "Shame she's too weak to do that now."

A hush settled over the group – laughter drained, replaced by an uneasy tension. Hazel ventured softly, "How's she doing?" She knew Janis didn't like to talk about serious things. In that regard, she'd found most boys were the same. It's why she liked Aspen; he seemed more serious, more... grown-up.

Janis's expression darkened. "Not great. Barely gets out of bed. But hey, she'll bounce back. I know it."

An awkward hush fell. That part of the conversation was over as far as Janis was concerned.

Eventually, Ava ventured, "I wonder what they wanted to recruit her for."

A faint breeze rustled the leaves overhead. Hazel and Ava exchanged glances. Wilder's name surfaced, along with murmured suspicions of bigger plots and bigger secrets. The man had disappeared a while ago, along with Aspen's parents. And before this, he had seemed so angry at the assemblies. He was right, of course – about the dwindling food supplies, the increasing droughts, their fragile future in the valley. And then he'd always go on those long hunts in the forests but rarely with anything to show for it.

Hazel, itching to push the subject away, gave the others a gently pleading look. "Hey guys, be absolutely honest." She paused. "You think Aspen might actually like me?"

Silence. Then Janis found a weak smile and topped off their cider. The river glinted, life meandering on with or without them. A gentle breeze carried the scent of wildflowers and uncertain dreams.

* * *

Old Mossbeard let out a gravelly sigh, muttering barely intelligible words that only those fluent in the peculiar language of the elderly might decipher. He stared at the steep path before him, brow furrowed with a mild dread, then took his first careful step onto the narrow trail.

Why, in the name of all things sane, had he agreed to this? On a perfect summer day, he should be back at the gardens, comfortably seated in a weathered chair beneath a sprawling oak, sipping cold cider and watching the younger folks sweat. Instead, he was trekking through the underbrush, out in the sweltering sun, once more trying to prove he wasn't too old for this nonsense. Not today, he thought. Maybe tomorrow, but not today.

The rocky, overgrown path twisted downward, the edges blending into wild forest without rhyme or reason. He'd walked this route countless times but had never felt so unsure of his footing. Perhaps Dawn was right – he shouldn't have done this alone.

He stumbled, cursing loudly, narrowly avoiding a tumble that could have claimed his life. How ironic would that be? Survive the Factory, the revolution, and every hellish chapter since, only to die chasing after some cocky teens in the woods. The thought rattled a laugh from him, which morphed into a coughing fit that sent birds flapping in alarm. A noble end indeed, he mused sourly. The ballad of Old Mossbeard, forgotten in the dirt.

He gathered himself, wiped his brow, and trudged forward. "Damn kids," he grumbled to the trees, bracing for each uncertain step.

* * *

Long hours passed beneath a searing sun – hours spent dozing on sun-warmed stones and halfheartedly casting lines into the lazy current. The sky's blazing eye was unrelenting as it drifted beyond noon.

Yet despite the heat, the river teemed with life. Tall grass on the banks shimmered like green-gold filaments, swaying in the breeze as if each blade harbored a tiny star. Birds flitted overhead, trading sweet melodies from branch to branch. A family of ducks paddled in leisurely circles, their downy young chasing rippling reflections on the water. The river itself glinted beneath that merciless light – a restless ribbon of liquid glass, tumbling on toward some distant, unreachable place.

Days like this made Ava, Hazel, and Janis feel invincible. They melded with the chaos and color of the world around them – ducks and deer, dragonflies and mosquitoes – and it all felt effortlessly right. Every so often, conversation fell silent whenever something wondrous caught their eyes: an eagle soaring across the snow-topped peaks, or the heavy tread of some unknown beast on the far riverbank. Isn't this – they always wondered – how life is supposed to be?

Yet beneath that sunlit surface, they sensed an unraveling. Each year brought fewer animals, feebler crops, harsher storms. The river ran thinner and often foul; the land itself seemed to wither. They noticed fewer ducklings than in summers past, a smaller brood than ever bobbing uneasily on the shallows. An unspoken dread lingered just beyond their collective awareness. So they did not talk about it.

Instead, they salted the single trout and left it in the sun to dry, then fled for sanctuary beneath a sprawling willow. The rustle of leaves and the lazy hum of flies set an almost dreamlike calm. Time ebbed away until they forgot about Aspen and his perfect hair, or Janis's bruised ego at the solstice festival, or Wilder's mysterious absences. For that moment, there was only tree and breeze and birdsong and grass – simple perfection. Why can nothing ever last?

They woke in the late afternoon light, faces warm, limbs languid with sleep. A twig snapped, pulling them from their doze. Then a gruff voice tore through the stillness.

"Hello!? Useless kids?"

Startled, they scrambled upright, hearts pounding.

"Mossbeard!" Hazel exclaimed, relief flooding her. The old man emerged from the shrubbery, moss and twigs clinging to his gray beard.

Janis flinched at the interruption, scowling. "Who you calling useless?" he said.

Mossbeard's weathered eyes narrowed beneath his bushy brows. Leaves dangled from his long, unkempt beard, his wool cloak stained by the trail's dust. He was breathing heavily, though he tried hard to hide it. Hazel noticed his knuckles go white on his walking stick – he was steadier when he had something to lean on.

"Ah, forgive me," he said, clearing his throat. "Thought you'd be further downstream. Anyway, pack up your things. Break time's over. Dawn needs help with the berry bushes, and I... volunteered to fetch you." His eyes sparkled with a wry amusement. "On account of my youthful vigor."

Janis rolled his eyes. "Sure thing. Sounds like fun. The thorns are the best. Let me grab our catch —"

"My catch," Ava corrected.

"Right, right. Her catch." He stuffed the salted fish into his bag. Mossbeard, meanwhile, stooped to pick something from the ground and pocketed it without explanation. Ava and Janis exchanged a shrug.

"Old folks," Hazel whispered with a grin. "Mysterious ways."

Mossbeard growled, though the corner of his mouth curled in a faint smile. "Now move along. Sun won't be up forever, and we've got work to do if we plan on surviving past next winter."

They gathered their gear – Ava unsuccessfully trying to conceal a pack brimming with empty bottles – and followed the old man back along the precarious forest trail. Soon the landscape opened into neat rows of fields and orchards, the scent of ripening fruit drifting on the breeze. The sun had begun its slow descent, gilding the world in pale gold. The low cluck of chickens drifted over from somewhere deeper in the village. Bees and flies buzzed lazily in the golden air.

Dawn greeted them with a tired but warm smile. She stood among the berry bushes, sleeves rolled up, sweat trickling down her brow. She was tall and strong – some said the valley would crumble without her grit and resolve. They all looked up to her, particularly the girls.

"Mossbeard, you made it back," Dawn teased. "Looking a bit ragged around the edges, though."

He grunted. "I'm alright, just old bones. Could be worse. I could be dead." A laugh bubbled from him, and he jabbed a gnarled finger at the trio. "Caught them napping, if you can believe it."

Dawn sniffed the air, eyebrows raised, but said nothing about the faint scent of alcohol. Instead, she filled them in on the day's task. "We hadn't planned on harvesting these berries so soon, but the weather forced our hand," she said, wiping her brow. "It's a gamble every season now. Fruit's rotting on the branches. Tough winter ahead if we don't salvage what we can."

She rattled off a few guidelines: pluck only the ripe ones, watch out for thorns, leave some for the birds – the cycle of life, after all, included them too. Once they'd stashed Ava's trout in a shed, the friends each grabbed a pair of shears and trudged over to the unpicked bushes. Dawn gave the fish a skeptical glance – its red lesions were unsettling, but she said nothing.

"Take care of them for me, Ava!" Dawn called.

"Gee, thanks, Mom," Janis muttered with a sarcastic snip of his shears. Hazel moved a bit away, unsettled by his sudden prickliness.

On the way, they encountered Rosemary, heavily pregnant and resting in a rickety chair while her husband Basil scoured the lower branches for hidden berries. Their five-year-old son Nettle bounded around, sticky fingers drawn to anything shiny.

"Hello!" he chirped. "Wanna play catch?"

Janis held up his shears. "Gotta work, little man."

Undeterred, Nettle peered at the shears until his mother warned him off. With a mischievous grin, he gave Janis the finger and darted away.

Basil sighed. "Sorry about that. Kid's been moody ever since we told him he's getting a sibling."

A yell sounded from somewhere among the bushes, "Hey! Give those back, boy!" and Nettle's giggles filled the air.

The three friends shared a look and pressed on. Clouds had begun to cluster overhead, sending a merciful breeze across the field. Old Mossbeard hauled a chair into the shade of a gnarled apple tree and sprawled comfortably, sipping water and calling out pointers.

"Watch the bottom of your baskets!" he barked. "Don't crush the good ones!"

They responded with the kind of exasperated groans only teenagers can muster, but Mossbeard simply chuckled, unconcerned. He drifted into one of his stories about the early days – when this valley was little more than a dream, when they'd first fled the Factory after the revolution, learning how to plant and forage by trial and error. The very word 'Factory' echoed a different era – a time of metal towers and harsh rules, shattered by the revolution they still half-whispered about in the valley. Almost none but old Mossbeard had been there.

"Without Ren, we'd have died," he said. "She stuck around when the other suits left. Taught us how to hunt, farm, fish. Lucky for us, she had all sorts of skills the others of her kind lacked." The mention of Ren always brought forth both wonder and a slight apprehension. They were so different, the suits, with their long limbs and curious apparatuses that could summon knowledge from thin air. Some said that Ren had played a crucial role in the revolution, but if she did, neither Mossbeard nor Ren herself ever mentioned it.

Martens, older and more inquisitive than he looked, sidled closer, bright red hair blending with his badly burned cheeks. Juice dribbled down his chin as he mumbled, "But how'd the other groups survive without her?"

Ava chimed in, "My mom told me that in the beginning, everyone shared knowledge. We sent folks to other communities, they sent people to us, and we exchanged tools, seeds – everything."

Mossbeard nodded. "Aye, child. Your mother's a wise one. Other groups also had suits of their own, some more competent than others. None like Ren though. And there were so many people then – too many to stay in one place." His breath hitched, and he coughed. "That was a different world, though."

"I don't like suits," Martens grumbled. "They give me the creeps."

"That's 'cause you're an idiot," Janis said. Martens lunged, tackling him in a quick scuffle – Dawn glanced over with a resigned sigh but didn't bother intervening. Eventually, Janis was forced to apologize and praise Martens's superior intellect.

Hazel let them wrestle, her mind drifting. "I wonder where Ren is now," she murmured softly. "We haven't seen her in ages."

Mossbeard's grin softened. "Likely hidden away in her little cabin. She'll return when she gets lonely – she always does."

His gaze swept over them like a protective father. Then he closed his eyes, letting the mild breeze wash over him. The sun was dipping low, painting the orchard in warm light. Everything seemed at peace, at least for now. And for a moment, that was enough.

CHAPTER 2

Deep within an ancient forest, many days' march from the valley, Ren found solitude – and she cherished every moment. She had never quite understood the need to anchor one's happiness to other people's presence. Here, in her sturdy little hut hidden among moss and ferns, she could study and observe in peace, liberated from the clamor of village life.

She'd built the hut herself, recalling the skills she had once shared with the valley's earliest settlers. At a glance, it resembled something lifted from an old fairytale – a witch's lair, tucked away from prying eyes. In truth, most folks in the valley found Ren a little frightening. She was tall, her limbs oddly long, her face different, and she appeared unexpectedly every now and then, like some wandering spirit. At least, she thought wryly, I don't eat children.

That afternoon, she sat on a makeshift bench outside her hut, watching squirrels dart through the greenery. A bird trilled overhead. Memories surfaced – of a distant revolution, of the day the Tower toppled, of the role she and her fellow suits had played in shaping a new world. Suits: humans who lived longer, remembered more, and sometimes wished they could forget. They had been bred for specific purposes – managers, technicians, advisers – but those lives had died with the Tower.

Solitude suited her. Nearly everyone who had witnessed the revolution was gone – either passed on or scattered to unknown corners of this earth. Only a few still lingered: Old Mossbeard, for one, still recounting half-remembered battles at every turn. Ren had stayed in touch with other suits now and then, but the once-thriving network connecting them was decaying – only a few satellites remaining, archives corrupted, entire chunks of human history erased like sand dunes in a storm. Each year her world shrank, pressed in on all sides by ancient trees.

She sighed. Over the decades, her visits to the valley had dwindled. The younger folk regarded her as some eerie figure from the dark woods, and she too felt oddly estranged from them. Yet she'd need to return soon, if only to check on Old Mossbeard and Fern – her onetime student, now the chronicler of a revolution that felt almost mythical to younger generations.

Restlessness filled her. Suits bored easily, so she picked up what the valley folk called a "shiny rectangle," her beloved tablet – a relic of the old world with its billions of stored books and games. She regularly cleaned and repaired it with salvaged tools from the Factory, but she knew its days were numbered, just as hers were.

Today, the screen bore grim tidings. Ren opened the weather forecast and stared at a swirling supercell system raging across the ocean, fueled by vast reserves of heat. In a matter of weeks, it would crash against the mountain ranges that sheltered the valley. If the storm's path remained true, the community was in serious danger.

Her hands trembled slightly. The valley had never faced anything quite like this. Yes, they knew droughts and brutal winters, but these new superstorms came from nowhere, sometimes swallowing half a continent before vanishing just as suddenly. The valley was ill-prepared: flimsy shelters, meager food reserves, and a population that had never experienced destruction on such a scale. Ren set her jaw. Better to warn them, she decided, than do nothing at all.

She shut off the tablet and rose, moving toward the squirrels. They'd grown accustomed to her presence, and she recognized each one by name. "Come here, Tony," she said softly, extending a walnut. The creature scampered up, took the prize, and retreated to boast among its peers.

Smiling, Ren stepped inside her hut. She gathered provisions – food, water, spare clothes, a knife, the precious tablet. Dusk had settled, but she intended to travel by moonlight, at least for a few hours. Her eyes roamed over the place one final time: the well-worn chair, the soot-darkened hearth, Ava's little wooden rabbit perched on a shelf. A part of her suspected she'd never see any of it again. That, in time, the forest would reclaim the beams and floors, leaving no sign of her existence. Her throat tightened at the thought; this hut was her anchor to the simpler life she'd built, a sanctuary from the world's horrors.

She shut the door and found the familiar trail. A swirl of memories from the community's first days enveloped her: huddled survivors of the Factory, forging a life against impossible odds. For a brief, shining moment, they had all been united – traumatized, yes, but bonded by shared hope. They had been a family, the only one she'd ever had.

Now, she wondered if they were beyond redemption – or if there was still a place in this restless world for them all.

* * *

Some summer days stretch on as though time itself has slowed, the sun lingering high above until it finally concedes to dusk. Today was such a day: the kind where you wake to warm light already bathing the world, and even as evening sets in, the heat still clings to every surface. Only when the sun at last crept below the mountains did a cooler breeze wander through the valley.

Ava, Hazel, and Janis had spent most of this enduring day hunched over thorny bushes, filling their baskets with berries of every color. By late afternoon, they'd delivered their haul to the shed, where Dawn and the others would see to sorting and canning. Then, the three friends trudged homeward – Ava's place tonight, for dinner with her parents.

Old Mossbeard, who had watched them work all day, decided to join them, naturally. He hadn't visited Ava's parents in ages, and besides, he hoped to taste her father's new brew rumored to have a delicate peachy twist. Ava, unwilling to confirm or deny anything, simply rolled her eyes at the old man's enthusiasm.

They strolled along a path alive with the low hum of crickets and the gentle rustle of leaves. Long shadows reached across the fields as the sunlight slowly faded behind jagged peaks, painting the air in orange-and-pink ribbons. Mossbeard moved with cautious steps, his face etched by fatigue, but he still managed a steady stream of jokes and anecdotes. Often they paused so he could greet a passing neighbor, boasting of their group's "heroic fishing" on the day before (although he'd had no part in it) and praising their baskets "brimming with sweet, sweet berries." Ava, Hazel, and Janis shared wry glances but said nothing. They knew Mossbeard had earned his small victories, many times over.

When they finally reached Ava's house, her parents, River and Fern, stood in the yard, visibly startled to see the old man tagging along.

"Mossbeard," River said, hesitating between a polite grin and a frown. "What a – uh – pleasant surprise. Didn't expect you tonight."

"Be nice," Fern chided, elbowing him.

"I am!" he insisted.

With a hearty laugh, Mossbeard shook their hands. "Came to sample some fresh trout – and, well, I heard rumors of a peach-laced beer, River. Couldn't pass that up, not with these old bones."

River flashed Ava a sharp look. She raised her hands. "I didn't tell him anything, I swear!"

Fern chuckled and waved them inside. "You're in luck, Mossbeard. We've plenty of fish – and apparently plenty of beer, too, judging by how our cellar smells."

They stepped into a warm, inviting space awash with the scents of freshly baked bread and pungent herbs. Outside in the yard, they set up a simple cooking area. River stirred the fire to the perfect intensity for grilling trout; Fern and the others chopped onions, peeled potatoes, and prepared a tangy berry sauce. Meanwhile, Old Mossbeard settled onto a bench with a mischievous twinkle in his eye, occasionally muttering into his beard. Whenever someone asked "What?" he'd respond "Huh?" – and that was usually the end of it. Occasionally, he'd rise to stretch and pick up something from the ground. He liked keeping odd mementos to remember the day by.

In time, the fish and sides were ready, and they gathered around a sturdy wooden table. The late evening sun skimmed the horizon in a haze of red and gold, cicadas humming their nightly tune. They ate mostly in companionable silence, soaking in the day's last warmth. Hazel, self-appointed gourmet, declared the trout crispy yet succulent, the berry sauce sweet but not cloying, and the potatoes perfectly buttery. Janis laughed for a full minute and mockingly teased her poetic flair, but soon mumbled his agreement, devouring the meal with both hands.

For once, Old Mossbeard spoke little. Then, as if unable to restrain himself any longer, he said, "This trout is the best I've had in years. We really outdid ourselves this time."

Janis lifted his gaze. "We? We didn't do anything. You just sat around and –"

Fern quickly interjected, pushing a stray lock of hair behind her ear. "It's all about timing," she said. "Catch 'em at the right moment, cook 'em at the right moment, and never forget the spices." She paused dramatically. "Not everyone realizes how vital spices are."

They all knew she was referring to Iris, the spice-averse neighbor whose culinary choices, among others, drove Fern half mad. A long-standing, friendly-but-irritated rivalry had evolved between the two women, though each insisted she was right. Mossbeard cut off the story before Fern got too worked up, waving a dismissive hand. "Yes, yes, the spices are perfect," he grumbled, leaning back with a sigh.

After some time spent trading gossip and small talk, Mossbeard suddenly perked up, pointing at River. "What about that beer, then?"

Janis jumped to his feet with mock drama. "Yes! The beer, man. We demand the beer!"

With a sigh and a grin, River disappeared into the basement, reemerging moments later with three wooden pitchers. Frothy, golden liquid sloshed to the brim. Each person poured a cup, took a careful sip, and gave a collective sound of approval – something between a hum and a sigh.

"Delicious," Fern said, swallowing another mouthful.

Janis nodded eagerly, echoed by Ava and Hazel. Mossbeard, however, downed his first cup in a single gulp, refilled it, then stood and paced the yard with a distant look, gazing at the darkening mountains.

"Mossbeard?" River ventured, brow furrowed with concern. "Everything alright?"

The old man paused mid-stride, took another swig, and rumbled a few indecipherable syllables before finally blurting, "This is the best thing I've ever tasted."

His eyes glistened, and he turned away. Hazel rose, gently resting a hand on his shoulder. "Mossbeard? What's wrong?"

He shook his head. "Nothing, child. Just an old man's memories. Live as long as me, and everything reminds you of the past."

Fern leaned in. "Anything you want to share?"

He hesitated, glancing from face to face as if weighing whether to unburden himself. "Might spoil the evening, is all..."

River shook his head. "We'd like to hear it, old friend. If you're willing."

They all knew Mossbeard's mood swings had grown more pronounced over the last months. Sometimes he vanished into his house, speaking to no one, lost in the shadows of the old Factory days. Tonight, he seemed willing to confide in a way that went beyond simple recounting of facts. Hazel took his calloused hand. "But only if you want to," she reminded him gently.

Slowly, Mossbeard returned to his seat. He sipped the last of his beer, savoring its subtle peach flavor. It reminded him of days long ago, when they first discovered the fruit – when Ren insisted it was safe to eat, and they gorged themselves until they nearly got sick.

"I've told you plenty about the Factory," he began, voice low and uneven. "How we drove back the Blackshirts, how Hammer led that final push, and Pascal's and Ren's plan that ended it all. But there are... pieces I left out. Pieces that plague me every night. Nightmares."

Fern exchanged an uneasy glance with River, well aware of the gaps in Mossbeard's stories. At last, she sighed and inclined her head for him to continue.

"I don't think I have much time left," he murmured, the weight of his years palpable in each word. "I'm ancient – second only to Maple, that old hag. She'll outlive us all with those radishes of hers. But me?" He gave a half-hearted chuckle. "I'm just grateful I got to spend my life here with you."

Hazel's eyes brimmed with sympathy. River lifted his cup in a silent toast.

Mossbeard set his hands on the table, fingers trembling. "I've told you many stories of the revolution. My humble part in it. But not this. I think it's time you learned the truth about me." He sucked in a breath. "Before the uprising, I had been... a gray soldier. I'd worked beneath the Tower. In the dungeons."

He paused, tears forming at the corners of his eyes. His voice began to shake.

"The things I've done..."

A hush fell, broken only by the buzz of insects and the crackle of the dwindling fire. Slowly, gently, they surrounded him, prepared for the tale they had never heard. And as the last bright sliver of sun vanished behind the mountains, the great darkness spilled from Mossbeard's memories – one that would change how they saw this gentle old man forever.

CHAPTER 3

To most in the community, the valley felt like the entire world – home to winding footpaths, sturdy wooden houses, fields brimming with produce, and wild meadows where nature persisted in tangled abundance. It was a swirl of dirt and beauty, civilization and wilderness, ruled by a few hundred spirited souls who liked to believe they were each extraordinary.

Among these souls was Aspen, son of Heather and Brook, known for his enviable looks and hair without a single frayed end. A heartthrob to many – male and female alike – he often seemed poised for a life of endless excitement. Yet on this particular day, nothing about his life felt grand. He lay sprawled in his stuffy bedroom, sweat trickling down his brow as he stared at the chipped and cracked ceiling. The heat pressed on him like an unwanted blanket. Let the sweat come, he thought. Let it fucking flow.

He usually passed dull afternoons letting his imagination roam through visions of a perfect future – one where he starred in every scene. But today, his thoughts kept drifting back to his parents' mounting absences. Heather and Brook were gone more often than not, disappearing for nights or even weeks, returning with feeble lies about "boar-hunting." Aspen was no fool. He knew they were hiding something. If it involved Wilder, it must be dangerous – and, therefore, exciting. I'm nearly a man, he thought. I should be part of this.

Agitated, he sat up, rubbed the sweat from his face, and padded downstairs in nothing but his skin. They weren't here to chastise him, so why bother with clothes? He prowled the silent rooms – kitchen, living space, an empty bedroom, a half-forgotten storage nook – flinging open windows in the hope of a breeze. He circled the rug, angry with himself for feeling so alone, so discarded. In a sudden burst of frustration, he punched the wall. A painting of storm-swept cliffs crashed to the floor, its frame splintering. Fuck, she'll be furious.

His heart thumped with raw energy, but the satisfaction of breaking something vanished quickly, leaving only the sting in his knuckles. As he shook out his hand, his gaze slid to the narrow door beside the fireplace. The basement. Maybe he'd poke around – anything to distract him. But just as he turned, a knock echoed from the front door.

He froze, hoping the visitor might give up. A moment passed, then the knock came again, louder this time.

Hazel braced herself on the doorstep, fidgeting with her shirt and fighting the urge to flee. You've come this far, she told herself. Don't run now. She clutched the hot raspberry pie, fresh from a morning's labor in her parents' kitchen, and tried to force a confident smile. Ava had warned her not to chase boys – "Let them come to you, be proud," Ava had said – but here Hazel was anyway.

The door opened. Aspen stood in the doorway, naked, scowling. Hazel's breath caught in her throat. The pie nearly slipped from her trembling grasp.

"Uh... hi, Aspen!" Her cheeks flared crimson, and she struggled to look anywhere but there. "I – I brought you this. A pie." The silence stretched as his glare seemed to pierce through her. "We had left-over raspberries, and I thought –"

Something flickered behind his eyes, and suddenly his whole demeanor shifted, like he'd remembered how to act in front of other people. "Oh. Yeah," he said. "Wow, thanks. Looks great."

Hazel gave a nervous laugh. "So, I guess you're... well, it's, um, hot in there?"

He merely shrugged. "Yeah. Thanks again, but – uh – I've gotta go. See you around." He nudged the door shut in her face.

Hazel stood there, pie-less, heart hammering. What the hell just happened? Did I imagine the whole thing? Was he really naked? She blinked at the closed door. Anger, shame, and shock mingled in her mind, threatening tears she refused to let fall. Ava had been right about not chasing after boys – but the damage was done now. Feeling absurd and humiliated, Hazel decided she needed a drink. Or three.

Aspen placed Hazel's pie on the table, popped a raspberry into his mouth, then turned back toward the small door by the fireplace. Candle in hand, he descended the narrow steps into the basement, where the smell of damp earth and mold clung to every surface. Unused onions and potatoes lay in corners, half-spoiled. Shelves and crates had been rearranged. Suspicious.

A prickle of excitement coursed through him. Something was off, and maybe this was the proof he needed. He combed the walls, brushing aside cobwebs, scattering startled bugs. At last, behind a heavy shelf, he found a narrow, hidden gap. With effort, he shoved the shelf aside and peered in.

His eyes widened. A secret room.

He crawled through the narrow opening. Bright, fresh wood smell hit him first – someone had installed brand-new shelves. And on each shelf rested row upon row of sleek metal shapes attached to wooden grips. Aspen ran a hand over one, feeling a slick, oily residue. Cold metal. A shiver of adrenaline sparked in his chest.

What the fuck is this?

* * *

His parents returned late in the evening with the same stony silence they always wore, offering not a word of explanation. But this time, Aspen refused to be brushed aside. He'd seen too much – found their secret stash of whatever-it-was. If they wanted to keep him in the dark, they'd have to do better than that.

He squared his shoulders, steadied his breath, and confronted them while they ate. "I've been down in the basement," he said, voice taut with adrenaline. "I found that hidden room with the metal tubes. What are they?"

For a few moments, neither parent spoke. Then his mother stood, her eyes gone wide. "What did you just say?"

Aspen's voice cracked but he forged on. "Those metal things... I –"

"What the hell were you doing down in the basement?" she snarled.

She towered over him. A flicker of regret moved across his father's face, but Heather's anger flared too hot. "You ungrateful little shit," she spat. "We've given you everything, and this is how you repay us? Snooping around – demanding answers? You deserve nothing."

He never saw her hand coming. The backhand sent him staggering, a shock of pain lighting up his cheek. Tears blurred his vision, and he barely registered his father stepping in.

"Heather, calm down," Brook pleaded, gently pulling her away. "We should've been more careful. It's not his fault."

She recoiled, lips curled in disgust. Aspen tasted blood in his mouth; he braced a hand on the back of a chair to keep from collapsing.

"Aspen. Stand." Brook's voice was low, oddly kind. Aspen pushed himself upright, forcing his eyes to stay clear of tears. "Maybe you're right," his father murmured. "Maybe you're old enough now to be... included."

Behind them, Heather barked a laugh. "Old enough? He wastes his days with those little whores from the community. He's weak. Spoiled. In the wilderness, he'd die within a week, and you know it."

"Maybe," Brook said quietly. "But we'll let Wilder decide. He's seen the rifles, Heather."

Aspen felt his father's hand on his shoulder, a strange attempt at reassurance before Brook announced he was turning in for the night. It left him alone with his mother. She glared, her breath still ragged from rage, and seized his chin in a bruising grip.

"If you breathe a word of this to anyone, I'll fucking kill you myself," she hissed.

He managed a mute nod, tears rolling unchecked down his face. Heather released him with a sneer and disappeared upstairs after Brook. Aspen slumped to the floor in the silent gloom, sobbing into the dust.

Two days passed in suffocating tension. Aspen barely slept, and when he did, nightmares jolted him awake. In the pitch-dark of early morning, his father roused him with a gentle shake. "Get dressed, son. We're going out."

"Where?" Aspen mumbled, still half-dreaming.

"The forests. Wilder will meet us there."

They set out at dawn, trekking along paths Aspen had never known existed. Brambles tugged at his ankles, and the clammy heat promised another scorching day. His mother was nowhere to be seen, and he was silently grateful. Brook seemed calmer, even placing a hand on Aspen's shoulder during a wide stretch of trail.

"She's on edge," he said. "But we both love you. You know that, right?"

Aspen only nodded; though relief uncoiled in his chest, shame trailed close behind.

By midday, they'd reached a small clearing and settled on a fallen log to share dried meat and bread. As Aspen swallowed a last bite, Wilder appeared, dark coat and all. Despite the blistering heat, he carried it like a badge of honor. Slung over his back was a long metal tube, the same kind Aspen had glimpsed in that hidden room. A rifle, he reminded himself.

"Morning, fellas," Wilder said, dropping onto the log beside Aspen. He yanked off his boots with a wince, unleashing a cloud of odor that made Aspen gag.

"Sorry," Wilder chuckled, though his eyes betrayed no real contrition. "Mind if I join?"

Brook nodded. While they ate and made small talk about the weather and the vanishing game in the forest, Aspen sat quiet. He felt an unsettling thrill at the sight of the rifle, half dread, half fascination.

When they finished eating, Brook rose, wiping crumbs from his pants. "I'm heading back. Aspen, you stay with Wilder. Do what he says."

Fear roiled in Aspen's stomach, but Wilder's booming laugh dispelled it, momentarily. "I don't bite," he said, clapping Aspen's back. "Not usually."

For an hour, Wilder showed Aspen how to disassemble the rifle, naming each piece like a sacred relic. He insisted Aspen touch every metal part, rest it in his palms, then fit it back into place.

"You can't wield power you don't understand," Wilder said, his voice nearly reverent. "My grandfather taught me that, though we had no real weapons back then. You're lucky, boy."

Aspen nodded, unable to decide if he felt lucky or terrified. His heart beat irregularly; this object in his hands radiated an uncanny chill.

"Why are you telling me all this?" he ventured at last. "Why do we have these rifles in our basement?"

Wilder offered a thin smile. "Not just in your basement. There are more – everywhere. But that's not for you to worry about yet. Now, come on. Let's see if we can put that new knowledge to use."

They hunted in near-silence for nearly two hours, following deer tracks that Wilder had spotted. Aspen's mind reeled with a flood of instructions: how to step lightly, how to notice subtle hints of movement, how the wind could betray or protect you. He tried to remember it all, tried to ignore the persistent knot in his gut.

Finally, they emerged on a small rise overlooking a meadow of daisies. A single deer stood grazing, the picture of tranquility. Sunshine glossed its tawny fur, and Aspen thought it looked impossibly serene.

Wilder eased to a crouch, gesturing Aspen to do the same. Then he drew the rifle and exhaled, calm as a statue. "Watch," he whispered.

A thunderous crack split the silence. The deer crumpled, half-kneeling before crashing onto its side. Aspen's world slowed, eyes riveted on the wounded creature as it kicked and moaned in agony, the ground around it staining red.

"Time to finish it," Wilder said, rising.

Aspen's stomach lurched as they advanced. The deer convulsed, its eyes wide with terror or disbe-lief – he couldn't decide which.

"Look at it, boy! Open your damn eyes!" Wilder snarled, dragging Aspen closer. "This is real life. Blood and guts. The price we pay to eat, to live."

Bile crawled up Aspen's throat. He wanted to turn away, but Wilder violently seized him by the shoulders.

"You think your life at home is real?" Wilder's glare pinned him in place. "You're weak. They're all weak. But I'll fix that. Straighten up."

He thrust the rifle into Aspen's hands. "Do it. End its suffering."

The deer shuddered, groaning wetly, and Aspen felt his tears break free. "I – I can't," he choked.

"Yes, you can," Wilder growled. "And you will."

A flash of steel. Wilder's knife pressed against Aspen's throat, sharp enough to draw a thin bead of blood. "Kill, or be killed. This is nature. This is the price you pay. This is how humanity got on top. Pull the fucking trigger."

With trembling arms, Aspen struggled to steady the rifle. The deer's gaze locked with his own, a final moment of silent pleading. His finger closed on the trigger, and the shot tore through the stillness. The creature's head snapped back in a spray of crimson.

Aspen staggered, drops of blood painting his face. He tasted salt and copper. Wilder whooped with glee, hauling Aspen into a one-armed embrace.

"There's your dinner, son!" Wilder crowed, his breath hot against Aspen's ear. "Welcome to the Eagles. Now your mother can finally be proud of something, eh?"

Aspen's body shook, tears and sweat mingling on his cheeks. He could still see the deer's eyes, and the echo of that helpless gaze seared into his mind. But Wilder's laughter thundered on, as if they'd just shared the world's grandest joke.

CHAPTER 4

Ava and Dawn stood at the edge of the fields, the early morning sky tinted by a bittersweet beauty. The morning sun sparkled on dew-slick leaves, a light breeze stirring the drone of insects and the chirps of birds. After weeks of stifling heat that had baked the ground and drained wells, they could sense relief in the air. Thick clouds gathered on the horizon, promising rain and renewal, and the earth hungered for it as much as the people did.

The two had been working since before sunrise, tending the communal fields at the valley's outskirts. Their foreheads glistened with sweat, their hands callused from plucking weeds in precise, rhythmic motions. Others moved nearby – families, neighbors, friends – some resting, some laboring. As usual, fieldwork was a shared endeavor. A few elders watched from shaded spots, passing out water and offering words of encouragement. By mid-morning, a group of children had arrived, shouting and laughing, occasionally riling the adults slogging through the dirt.

Dawn, whose calm authority guided much of the farming and orchard tasks, glanced at Ava. The girl's face had gone pale; sweat dampened her short, unruly curls. She pressed her lips tight, as if to suppress some discomfort.

"Ava, you alright?" Dawn asked. "You look a bit off."

Ava exhaled. "I'm fine, just... had a rough night." She avoided Dawn's eyes.

"I was surprised to see you out here so early. Don't you usually help your mother with the archives?" Dawn paused, eyeing the building storm clouds overhead. "Come on, let me help you back –"

"No, no," Ava said, forcing a smile. "I'm good. Promise. I want to help, do something. Just need some water."

Dawn frowned but said nothing more. In truth, Ava's queasy state had little to do with heat or dehydration and everything to do with the cider she'd shared with the others the previous night. Hazel had been there, and Janis, and Martens, and some others too. Her attempt to mask a hangover wasn't fooling Dawn, who suspected as much, but chose not to pry. They carried on in mutual silence, pulling weeds and half-listening to the children's shrieks of joy. Nettle, the unruly son of Rosemary and Basil, was terrorizing people again with sticky fingers and unrelenting energy.

An hour later, the sky turned ominously dark. Drops of rain plunked down in scattered rhythms, then multiplied into a warm torrent that drenched the fields. People cried out in relief, tipping back their heads to let the water wash over them – but some of the elders eyed the clouds with worry. A sun-baked land could only absorb so much before flooding took hold.

A simple kind of magic, Dawn thought as she watched the people slowly disperse. The days were still warm, but as summer drew to a close something else crept in. Leaves would soon begin their slow transformation to shades of copper, while the occasional crisp breeze already carried the first melodies of the coming frost and all the hardships it would bring. It made her anxious and slightly melancholic.

"Let's get indoors," Dawn said quietly to Ava as the skies opened. The two made for Dawn's cabin perched on a small hill, just beyond the fields.

Ava dragged her feet, looking paler than ever, but managed a nod. She blamed bad food when Dawn asked about her condition again, but Dawn remained unconvinced. The pounding in Ava's head only grew worse with each step, and the sense of foreboding she'd harbored for days swelled in her chest.

They reached the cabin in a downpour. Dew greeted them on the porch with a teasing grin. "You sure know how to track mud, ladies. My poor porch."

"Our porch, you mean." Dawn smirked as Dew planted a kiss on her lips.

Inside, the cabin felt cozy – dry air tinged with the scents of tea and freshly cut herbs. Ava all but collapsed at the small kitchen table, trying to gather herself while Dawn and Dew bantered about the storm. Her stomach lurched, and she pressed her hand to her mouth.

"What's up with her?" Dew whispered to Dawn. She set three cups of tea down and rummaged through her medicine pouch.

"It's either blood or booze," Dawn said, only half joking. "Maybe both."

"Thought so," Dew replied, unearthing a small vial of bitter liquid. She offered it to Ava. "Drink this. It'll help."

Ava grimaced at the first swallow. "I'm not hungover," she lied weakly.

Dew's raised brow said otherwise. "Hazel came by earlier looking just as green. You must've had quite a night."

Ava's protest died on her tongue. Dawn and Dew exchanged a knowing look, then let the matter drop – though not without a few teasing remarks. As they sipped tea, the rain intensified into a rapping staccato on the roof. Wind rattled the window frames.

For a while, Dawn and Dew talked shop: fields, animals, looming tasks. Ava listened, gripping her cup with shaky hands and battling nausea. She couldn't stop thinking about Hazel's heartbreak over Aspen – or the creeping dread that had been a constant shadow in her mind. Something felt off in the valley, something bigger than any of them. The gossip about Aspen's erratic behavior and all the rumors about Wilder and the others stuck in her head like a thorn.

She let her gaze drift to the window, raindrops blurring the view of rolling clouds. What's brewing out there? she wondered.

Eventually, Dew excused herself to organize supplies in the adjacent room. Now's my chance, Ava thought. I need to ask.

"Dawn?" she said, lowering her voice.

Dawn looked up from her tea. "Hmm?"

"Do you... know much about Mossbeard's past?"

Dawn's expression shifted. "He tells his war stories to anyone who'll listen. Why?"

"That's not what I mean," Ava said quietly, leaning in. "Has he mentioned... what he did in the dungeons? Beneath the Tower?"

Dawn hesitated, glancing toward the other room to ensure Dew was out of earshot. At length, she sighed. "He told me. Not everything, but enough. He believes people should know the truth before he goes. I don't blame him, and you shouldn't either. The man's carried that burden long enough."

Ava nodded, feeling a pang of guilt. "I don't. Blame him, I mean. It's just... well, he mentioned some old weapons. Rifles. They're very powerful and..." She trailed off, swirling her tea. "Did he ever tell you about that part?"

Dawn's brows furrowed. "No, he didn't. But Ren told me long ago, so I'm aware. Why do you ask?"

Ava took a breath and recounted what she'd experienced in the forest weeks before, the memory as clear as the thunderclaps rumbling outside. She'd been out collecting herbs on a blazing hot day – one of those summer afternoons when the world seemed to sleep under the sun's weight. Then, a series of deafening bangs had shattered the stillness. She'd frozen, unsure if she'd imagined it, until she'd stumbled upon a bloody patch of grass where an eagle feasted on a decapitated deer. Voices had floated through the woods, deep and urgent. One of them she could have sworn belonged to Aspen.

Dawn listened, eyes locked on Ava's. "And you never told anyone?"

Ava shook her head, warmth flooding her cheeks. "I didn't know what it meant. I was afraid it'd sound crazy. But... now everything lines up. Those strange noises, these rifles, Aspen's weird behavior. It can't be a coincidence."

Dawn set her mug aside and stared out at the storm-lashed hills. Outside, lightning branched across the dark sky, followed by a rumble that shook the cabin. *What are you up to, Wilder?* she wondered silently, and not for the first time. *And how deep into the shadows has Aspen been lured? Poor boy,* she thought.

Uncertainty crowded her thoughts. Rain hammered against the cabin walls as if demanding entrance, and Ava's voice trembled when she finally spoke again: "Dawn, what do we do?"

Dawn closed her eyes, inhaling the sharp tang of brewing herbs. She didn't have an answer that could dispel the dread. Outside, the thunder roared, and inside, the two friends exchanged a look that said something was coming – something they might not be able to stop.

CHAPTER 5

Two men hurried along the muddy path, dodging puddles and slick patches as best they could. The rain had eased into a chilly drizzle – no longer the downpour of earlier days, but still oppressive enough to keep spirits low. Weeks of gloom had settled over the valley, and the sun's fleeting appearances offered little comfort. The people had grown restless.

Moose, the bald, talkative one, was surprisingly cheerful despite the dreary conditions. He enjoyed a friendly chat more than anything and hoped this "secret assembly" might offer both conversation and, if fortune favored him, a bit of drink. His younger companion found the man's endless questions exhausting.

"You know what this assembly's about, lad?" Moose asked for the third time.

"No," replied the younger man. "As I've said, I know as much as you do."

Moose nodded, undeterred. "Curious, though, isn't it? Wilder asking us all here – unusual, if you ask me."

"Yes. Very curious," the younger man echoed, managing a polite smile through gritted teeth.

They sidestepped a large puddle, then another, but the younger man's foot slipped and his sock soaked through. He sighed, longing for a warm fire and silence. Moose, oblivious to his companion's misery, rambled on.

"Well, what do you suppose –"

"I have no idea, Moose," the younger man cut in. "Truly."

Moose just chuckled. "Aye, aye."

Seconds later, Moose skidded on a slick spot and grabbed the younger man's shoulder for balance. They both flailed in a bizarre, mud-spattered dance before pitching forward in a graceless heap. The earth swallowed them with a wet smack, leaving them coated from head to toe.

It was a full two minutes – and a string of curses – before they pushed onward, caked in muck and shivering in the damp.

"Almost broke me back there," Moose remarked at last, breaking a brief silence.

"Indeed," was all the younger man managed.

"How's your back, lad? Sore?"

"I'm fine," he muttered. "Thank you for asking."

Moose nodded, satisfied. "What about your feet? Wet, are they?"

"Yes," the younger man said, suppressing a tremor of rage.

"Dangerous business, cold feet. Could catch a chill."

"Quite," he agreed, desperate for an end to this conversation.

At last, they reached a stand of trees, and beyond it loomed Wilder's cabin – a sight that promised warmth and the company of others. Heather stood at the entrance, her expression hovering between amusement and disdain.

"What happened to you two? Decide to wrestle in the mud? Have some fun before the meeting, eh?" she said.

Moose puffed up. "Well, now, that's a curious stor–"

"I'd rather not talk about it," the younger man cut in quickly. "Could we go inside?"

Heather rolled her eyes and thrust an oily rag at them. "Clean off your boots and clothes first. Try not to fuck in the mud again."

Moose let out a hearty laugh and clapped his muddy hand across the younger man's back. The younger man winced, quietly praying for the day to be over. They wiped themselves down as best they could, then stepped into the crowded interior. Immediately, the younger man tried to lose Moose in the bustle, but Moose cheerfully plopped down in the seat right beside him.

"Let's see what Wilder's got in store for us, eh?" Moose said, grinning.

"Yes," the younger man murmured, noticing his hand trembling. "Let's see."

Moose elbowed him lightly. "Think they'll serve any cider or beer?"

A wave of longing hit the younger man – the urge to drive his fists into Moose became almost overwhelming. Yet memories of his late grandmother's final plea for politeness and restraint held him back. Moose had been a close companion of his grandfather as he'd drunk himself into an early grave. Some say he'd even encouraged his grandfather's drinking. "Perhaps afterward, Moose. Perhaps afterward."

"Aye," Moose said, grinning. "Let's hope so."

Within minutes, Moose held an oversized cup of steaming mulled wine. He grinned from ear to ear.

* * *

A row of tall candlesticks cast an eerie glow across Wilder's weathered features as he surveyed the gathering in his living room. Twenty-three people – handpicked by him – had squeezed inside, crowding chairs and benches, a few leaning against walls.

Brook and Heather stood by his side; Aspen hovered between them, shifting uneasily. Behind them, Wolf loomed like a statue, his expression unreadable.

"Friends," Wilder said, his voice carrying over the subdued murmur. "I appreciate you coming here." At once, the room fell silent, every eye turning toward him. "I know rumors have been swirling about what we've been up to." He motioned toward Brook and Heather, and by extension, Aspen. "But I promise: tonight, you'll understand everything."

He swept his gaze across the room, pausing on each face. Let them wait, his grandfather had once taught him. Let them get hungry for your words. Outside, the wind rattled the window frames, while inside, the rich aroma of the mulled wine hung in the air – wine he'd deliberately served to warm and soften them. Now, they were primed to listen.

"Tonight," he declared, "I'll tell you how we, all of us gathered here, will lead the valley into a brighter future."

Brook, following Wilder's lead, thrust a fist into the air. "Yes!" he roared, urging the others to respond.

A ripple of cautious approval spread. Someone clapped softly; a bald man – Moose – turned to the young man beside him, red-shot eyes gleaming with excitement. The younger man edged away, glancing down at the mud still caked on his shoes.

Wilder's tone softened as he spread his arms wide. "Don't you all love the valley? Don't you want your children to grow up somewhere safe, without dreading hunger every winter?"

Some nodded, uncertain yet hopeful. A woman raised her hand. "Of course we do. We just... it's the storms, the droughts, the... emptiness. The crops fail. The game is scarce."

"Yes," Heather said, gripping Aspen's shoulder in a way that made him flinch. "What we want is a future for our children. Not this poverty." She spat the last word.

Wilder hammered his fist on the makeshift podium. "And what if I told you we could have real safety? Real comfort? We wouldn't have to beg or rely on so-called 'communal shares.' We'd each have our own stockpiles, our own animals, our own tools – no more free-loaders riding on our backs!"

A wave of agreement swept the crowd. Moose leapt to his feet, coat still dripping from outside, nearly swatting the younger man's face with a soggy sleeve. "Hear, hear!" he shouted.

"Sit down, Moose," someone growled. "We can't fucking see."

Wilder smiled, letting the energy build. "Who here remembers the Factory?" he asked quietly.

Silence. A few looked down at their cups. An older man – Cedar – cleared his throat. "I do," he said, voice trembling with both pride and nerves.

"Tell us about it," Wilder coaxed, voice thick with reverence. "Tell us how it really was, not those tired stories from Old Mossbeard and Maple."

Cedar's eyes gleamed. "Well, the Factory had strict rules. You break 'em, you get punished. But if you just did your job, it was... it was all right." He paused, letting the memory settle. "There was a big tower, gold and diamonds on top. Many other grand buildings, too. And there was order. Everyone knew their place."

"Order," Wilder repeated, nodding meaningfully at the crowd. "Look at us now – leaderless, descending into chaos. Starvation, insecurity, a life with no discipline or structure! Right now, my friends," he said, "we are ruled by no one! And hence, we are ruled by chaos!" He glared at his audience, fist raised. "The valley is facing starvation and death, and there is no one to lead us! No one to tell the truth! No one to tell them" – he motioned vaguely at the windows – "what to do! They think they can keep us down; they think they can make us live like beasts, devoid of law, culture, and order! They're wrong, are they not?"

The reaction was immediate. A surge of angry cheers, fists pumping the air. Even Aspen found himself shouting along, though confusion swirled in his mind. Life in the valley isn't perfect, he thought, but we've never starved. Yet seeing his father and mother so riled, hearing Wilder's impassioned cries, he couldn't help but be swept along.

Wilder raised his hands, silencing the room. "We must reclaim our destiny – the destiny they denied us! The Factory might be gone, but its spirit lives on in us. We are its rightful heirs!"

More applause, louder now. A man near the back whooped in excitement; others joined. Wilder nodded to Brook, Heather, and Wolf, who vanished into the basement. They returned moments later, heaving a heavy bundle draped in tattered blankets.

"This" – Wilder yanked the cloth aside with dramatic flair – "is our path to security. To order. To prosperity."

A collective gasp swept the crowd. Beneath the blankets lay long metal tubes, neat rows of them. Gasps turned to awed whispers as Brook and Heather lifted a few, passing them around so each person could feel the cold metal. Wilder explained what they were and how they could be used. Aspen shivered, recalling the day he held one under Wilder's watchful eye. They're real, he thought, and terrifying.

"The time to use these will come," Wilder said gravely, "but not yet. You must not tell anyone outside this room. We must be cautious; we're still outnumbered by those who would cling to their old ways. But when the moment arrives –"

He lifted one rifle high, the flames from the fireplace dancing across its barrel. "We will restore law and order to the valley! We shall call ourselves the

Eagles – free as those who rule the sky, but here to reign on the ground!"

Roars of approval shook the small living room. Twenty fists shot into the air. Brook and Wolf bellowed something incomprehensible, and Heather let out a fierce cry. In the back, two or three remained uncertain, one quietly slipping out the door. Wilder noticed, filing away the detail for later. They'll need persuading, he told himself. He'd bring Wolf along; and Aspen, perhaps.

"Like Hammer before us, who was betrayed by Pascal and the suit scum," Wilder thundered, "we'll claim what's rightfully ours! The Tower! The Factory! The valley! We will rebuild! Everything!"

The walls reverberated with cheers. Moose leaped to his feet again, nearly toppling over in excitement. Aspen stood rooted to the spot, heart pounding. A thousand questions and doubts churned inside him, but still he raised his voice, echoing the chants his father led:

"Long live the Eagles!"

"Long live Wilder!"

Over the clamor, Wilder's grin grew feral. He had them in the palm of his hand now – twenty men and women chanting for war, or something like it. Aspen pressed himself against his father's side, uncertain, yet powerless to resist the frenzy. They can't all be wrong, he told himself. It must be true.

All the while, the rifles gleamed beneath the flickering candlelight. And in the hush between roars, a deeper darkness seemed to stir – one that had always been there, and always would be.

AUTUMN: CHAPTER 6

Old Mossbeard sat by the hearth, the steady crackle of flames blending with the rhythmic drum of rain outside. Autumn had crashed into the valley with uncanny speed – each year seemed to spin faster than the last, leaving him breathless at how soon the harvest loomed. Surely, he mused, we only planted those seeds yesterday?

He shuddered. A pang of melancholy crept under his skin, worse than any autumn he could recall. He felt ancient, so incredibly old. Not even before their first winter in the valley – so many years, decades, lifetimes ago – had he known such dread. It was as though Death itself stood behind him, cold fingers gripping his shoulders, urging him into a darkness he couldn't bear to face.

He jerked awake from the spiraling thoughts, heart thudding. Steady now, he told himself. It's not even winter yet. Time enough for madness once the real cold arrived. He rose from the chair, every joint protesting, then sank right back down, glaring at the fire for a moment. Is this what the old do? he thought. Sit staring at dancing flames until their eyes burn?

He coughed a brittle laugh. After everything he'd survived, after all the blood and toil, he was still here. Why me? he wondered, remembering the countless comrades who hadn't made it. Did they understand, as they died, what had been taken from them – and all that might have been?

His gaze flicked to the fire as it crackled. It reminded him of the hope they'd once shared in the valley, back when love and unity had bound them all. That love still exists, he told himself, but it's diluted now – churned by uneasy whispers and quiet rumors. Strange gatherings. Strange talk of a return to an older, crueler way.

He rubbed his beard and sipped lukewarm tea. A gust of wind rattled the windows, setting the flames dancing shadows across his lined face. He'd sensed it coming for months. The rumors of discontent, the whispered tales of secret groups, command structures, rifles. Dawn had mentioned thunderous booms echoing from deep within the forests, and Mossbeard knew all too well what could make such noise. He recalled the horrors and the hideous sense of power they granted:

– splattered flesh, red-soaked earth, shrieks, the scurry of fat rats, always that blinding smoke –

He forced the memory aside, focusing on the trees bent beneath the storm outside. Each day was a fresh battle – just as it was for the leaves, now turning copper and gold. They fluttered on fragile stems, fighting the season's inevitable decay. They won't win. Neither will I, he reflected. In the end, all must surrender to the cold.

His thoughts drifted, sliding into half-dreams. And suddenly he was gray and nameless again, entombed in the Factory's dungeons. Screams reverberated through those corridors. The stink of filth and terror filled every breath. Chains clanked on cold stone while suits with hollow smiles demanded unspeakable acts. A swirl of horror tensed his body until he jerked awake, soaked in sweat, tears winding through the tangles of his beard.

Remember who you are, he told himself. Mossbeard. Old Mossbeard.

He clung to a distant memory...

They were celebrating Ava's fifth birthday – a day when every child chose a name to keep for five years. More than a hundred people had gathered under a bright sky. Fern smoothed her daughter's hair, trying not to look too anxious.

"Have you decided, honey?"

"Yes!" the girl cried, voice trembling with excitement. "I want to be Ava!"

The crowd cheered. Dawn and Dew smiled, while River lifted his daughter so everyone could applaud the newest full member of the community. From that moment on, the girl could speak and decide for herself – within reason. Her parents would guide her, but the path was hers to walk.

Old Mossbeard (though he'd gone by a different name then) approached, knees creaking, heart warm. "A beautiful name. Where did it come from?"

"It's from a story Mom told me!" Ava beamed. But then she pointed. "Hey! There's something in your beard!"

He fished around and pulled out a tuft of green. "Moss, must've gotten caught on me."

A boy named Horse – eight years old, soon to pick a new name (Janis, to his mother's relief) – crowed with laughter. "Mossbeard! Mossbeard! You're a mossbeard!"

And the name stuck. Over time, someone tacked on "Old," and that was that.

The fire hissed again, pulling him back to the present. Old Mossbeard rubbed his eyes, stiff and sore. No, he was real, the valley was real, and those dungeons belonged to another life – one he refused to let taint this place.

He stood and stared out the window at the downpour. Then, with a grunt, he pulled on his boots and coat, grabbing a shovel. There were things to do, lines that must never be crossed again, old evils he wouldn't let fester here. The Factory lived in his nightmares, but the valley was his heart.

He was Old Mossbeard, and though he was battered, he could still play a part in protecting what remained.

Now, he thought, where did I bury them?

* * *

The weather was merciless, and so was the trail – treacherous underfoot, riddled with puddles and slick mud. Ren pressed on regardless, a thin silhouette in the storm. Wind rattled the canopy, sending leaves, twigs, and entire branches crashing around her. More than once, the flying debris struck her numb face and left her muttering half-comical curses, one of her favorite refrains being, "Why am I doing this?"

Lightning flared, revealing the towering trunks swaying overhead. Perfect, she thought. Just perfect. She was soaked to the bone, shivering so hard it felt like her teeth would crack. Suits were made for maneuvering in industrial complexes and surviving on minimal calories, not for braving autumn storms in a sodden forest. Her boots felt like lead, toenails floating somewhere in the puddled insides. She should have reached the valley a week ago.

Another fork of lightning carved the sky, followed by a thunderous crack. Ren staggered at a sudden gust of wind and toppled into a slushy pool of mud. The impact knocked the breath out of her, and she lay there, blinking up at the frantic dance of branches. A warm fire, she told herself. A good book, Tony the squirrel on my lap... She gritted her teeth, pushing away the notion that she might never see Tony again, or any of his furry kin.

She hauled herself upright, water streaming down her clothes. Left foot. Right foot. And then she saw it – a new blockade, a jumble of fallen trees and boulders deliberately set to block the path. Rage flared, mixed with primal terror. "Again?! Come on!"

Any squirrels that might have overheard her outburst were safely hidden from the gale, and the roar of the wind swallowed her voice anyway. She glared at the obstacle. Clearly, someone had made it their mission to seal off all routes into the valley save the mountain passes – a path almost impossible in such weather.

Who's doing this? Her fury brewed in her chest. Why isolate the valley now? She examined the barrier. No way around it – attempting to climb the slippery logs would risk a broken neck on the ravine's edge. She let out a guttural scream that would've frightened any wary souls who still mistrusted suits. Then she turned back. Again, she'd retrace her steps for days, losing precious time the valley no longer had.

Despite exhaustion, she marched. She needed a plan. The storm swelled with every gust, water saturating the brittle earth until any heavier downpour would trigger floods. Houses, crops, even entire families would be washed away. People might think the storm would soon pass, but Ren had the data: it wouldn't. They needed to leave, but where to go?

Her tablet chimed, weak and tinny. She'd set an alert to ping whenever it managed to connect to the decaying network. Usually that happened on a crest or hilltop, but sometimes it seemed random. Battery was dangerously low – no sun in weeks meant no reliable recharging. Still, she had to check the weather data. No surprise: type 7 storm on the way, with predicted flooding, gale-force winds, and little chance of easing. A heavy sigh escaped her. She slumped against a dripping trunk, rain drumming on her hood.

There was one last option – one she'd been mulling for days. Risky. Improbable. But the new barricades forced her hand; she wouldn't reach the valley in time, and they wouldn't evacuate on their own. If she arrived too late, they'd face the fury of autumn storms, minimal supplies, and impassable mountains. Certain disaster.

No other communities lingered to the east, south, or west. Most had gone north long ago, hoping for better conditions. Maybe that was still a possibility. They'd need an ally halfway – someone with rations and shelter. The valley was lost. They must flee northward, straight through the vast mountain ranges, where packs of wolves would pick them off one by one – if they didn't starve first. Their only chance was a group with supplies meeting them halfway. Ren steadied herself, opened her tablet, and typed a brief message:

Lightning pulsed, thunder bellowed. She glimpsed a tree exploding into splinters nearby, flames doused instantly by the torrent. At least there'd be no wildfires this time, she thought wryly, tucking the tablet away. She resumed trudging, drenched and trembling, pulse thrumming with a long-familiar tension. Fear. She rarely admitted to such a feeling, but here it was, gnawing her edges.

For decades, contact between communities had almost vanished. Once the survivors had parted ways after the Factory's fall, they'd scattered in all directions: hundreds here, thousands there, sometimes only dozens. Most suits, too, had gone off on their own. Ren had considered traveling south to study life's final battle against encroaching deserts, but she'd stayed, offering knowledge to help the valley's people survive. She remembered those first harmonious years – everyone recovering from physical and mental scars, forging a life together. But autonomy carried deep challenges, and old frictions eventually sparked. The "division" came, scattering them all. Peacefully, yes, but also irrevocably.

Now the fruit of that division was bitter. No allies. No sense of what lay beyond the horizon. She plodded through mud, lost in thoughts of 'what if,' 'we should have,' and 'maybe.' Too late. They were strangers now, if they even existed.

A fresh crash of thunder shattered her reverie. The storm crept closer. Ren imagined the message she'd sent blinking somewhere in the void. Who might answer? And would they come in peace, or with weapons? She'd seen humans at their worst – desperate, irrational, violent. Suits even more so, in their own ways. But no matter. The valley's survival depended on taking the risk.

Her tablet buzzed softly. A response? Already? Ren's heart skipped. Anxiety flooded her veins. She

forced herself to walk another hour before daring to
read it.

CHAPTER 7

Dew ground herbs at the kitchen table, her arm muscles tensing with every turn of the pestle. Hazel sat close by, dreading whatever bitter concoction her headache would require. The oppressive humidity and unending rainfall had the valley on edge, and Hazel felt its weight acutely.

"So," said Dew, pressing down on the mixture and recounting the familiar story once more. "Let me see if I've got this right. You baked a pie and took it to him?"

Hazel nodded. "Yes."

"And he answered the door" – Dew's tone was playful – "completely naked?"

Hazel flushed, catching Ava snickering in the next room. "Well... yes."

"You saw his –"

"Dew!" Hazel shot her a mortified glare.

"But yes," Hazel added quietly. "I did."

"And then he just snatched the pie from you?"

"That's right," she said, wincing at the memory. "I mean –"

"And later," Dew continued, her eyebrows lifted in mock astonishment, "after weeks of no contact, you made him another pie?"

Hazel sighed. "When you put it like that, it sounds pathetic."

"Mm-hmm. And he yelled at you?" Dew set down the pestle, gaze probing. Hazel looked away, embarrassed at the recollection.

"Yeah."

"That little shit," Dew hissed. "We ought to pay him a visit and –"

A furious banging on the front door cut her off. "Dew!" a shrill voice called. "Are you there? We need help! Please!"

Dew glanced at Hazel. Ava put aside her book, following Dew as she hurried to the door. It flung open to reveal Nettle – soaked to the bone, eyes wild with fear.

"Nettle, what's wrong?" Dew knelt, grasping his shoulder.

"M-My mom," he stammered between shudders. "She – she's having the baby, but – there's so much blood."

Dew's expression darkened. "It's too soon," she muttered. "Ava, grab my bag from upstairs. Hazel, you're with me. Come on!"

Within moments, they were racing out into the rain, Hazel leading the trembling boy by the hand. The downpour soaked them in seconds, but none slowed. They needed to reach Rosemary's house – where new life battled to enter the world.

At roughly the same time, Dawn stood in the rain, rubbing her cold-numbed fingers and worrying about the coming winter. Over the last few weeks, the valley's weather had grown perilously out of season – too much rain, too much chill, far too soon. She glanced over at Birch, who waited beside her.

"You ready?" he asked softly.

"No," she admitted, "but let's get it over with."

They trudged out into the waterlogged fields. Dawn stepped where Birch's boots left deep imprints in the mud, using them as makeshift footholds. Visibility was minimal – fog and heavy rain concealed most everything – but what little they could see looked grim. It was a graveyard. Stooping to inspect the first row of crops, Dawn's chest tightened. The soil was saturated, plants suffocating in black sludge.

"How bad?" Birch asked, fiddling nervously with his whiskers. A weathered man in his fifties, he'd seen his share of disasters, yet he looked pale now.

Dawn didn't answer. Off to the right, crows pecked hungrily at the ground, flapping sodden wings. She stared at them dully, lacking the will to chase them off. Further along, the leaves drooped, their color fading to a sickly yellow. They're ruined, she thought. Lifting her eyes to the leaden sky, she could only murmur, "Stop. Please."

But the rain persisted. They moved methodically from row to row, confirming the same grim truth, until no doubt remained.

A small crowd had gathered in front of Rosemary and Basil's home, huddled under a canopy of firs. Rain battered the cabin's roof, draining off the eaves in overflowing rivulets. They eyed Dew with desperate relief the moment she arrived. She always had a solution – just like her mother once had.

Dew burst inside with Ava, Hazel, and Nettle close behind. The leaks in the ceiling were caught in pans, and the single fire in the hearth barely provided light or warmth. In the flickering glow, Rosemary lay in bed, gasping in agony, sheets soaked red. Basil stood at her side, trembling and speechless.

"Everyone out!" Dew barked. "Now!"

Those who lingered vanished at once, leaving only the necessary few. Old Maple, a veteran of many births, approached Dew, face etched with concern. "It's not good," she whispered. "Too much blood. I fear –"

Dew offered no reply, turning instead to Rosemary, whose screams had grown faint. Basil, stoic, clutched her hand. A younger woman, Dandy was her name, wrists and fingers stained with blood, explained they'd tried to stop the bleeding. It kept coming. Dew administered a strong dose of painkiller, and Rosemary's cries soon subsided to dazed murmurs.

"Basil," Dew said quietly, forcing the word from her throat.

He nodded, eyes on his wife's pale face. "I know. Just... save the child if you can."

Steeling herself, Dew let the numbness set in – a technician's detachment. Think of the cogs in the Factory, she told herself. Precision, no emotion, just motion.

"Ava?" she called.

"Y-Yes?"

"I need the big knife from my bag."

Ava fumbled, opening the brown satchel. Basil's voice murmured comfort to his wife, who smiled weakly back at him.

* *

By the final field, Dawn and Birch were drenched and hollow-eyed. Crows argued overhead, their caws sounding like mocking laughter. Dawn rested a moment, gazing at the wasted rows of crops. She'd weathered many trials before, but never such devastation. How could they feed the community now?

Birch's posture slumped. He asked no questions because they both knew the answer. Everything's lost. The wind carried the clatter of brittle leaves, a quiet lament in the face of unrelenting rain. Dawn thought of Dew – always so hopeful – and of the children, the elderly, everyone placing faith in them. But the harvest was gone. The valley's future grew darker by the day.

Still, she refused to surrender. Better to fight and lose than never to have tried, she reasoned. Better to struggle as free people than live the chain-bound existence from before. Drawing on that belief, she managed a weak smile. Birch noticed, confused, but as she enfolded him in a brief, reassuring hug, he relaxed. They'd face it all together. As a community.

They would not give up. They would survive, they always did. And if, by some chance, they did not this time, then they'd been alive at least.

Silence.

The newborn lay limp in Dew's arms, its tiny body lifeless and cold as winter ice. Tears streamed down Dew's face as she attempted, again and again, to coax a breath. It did not come.

On the bed, Basil held Rosemary's lifeless form, tears staining his cheeks. She was gone, too. The women in the room stood in numb shock, tears mingling with the ceaseless drip of rain outside. Ava knelt in a corner, face buried in her hands, Old Maple's trembling arm around her shoulders. In the other room, Hazel murmured consolation to Nettle, who would never know his sister.

They wrapped the child in Rosemary's motionless arms and drew a blanket over them both. Nettle managed a tearful goodbye, and the rest could do little but stand by, hearts bruised and raw. Outside, the storm raged, wind rattling the windows as candles flickered in vain. Death had come, final and absolute. Uncaring.

* * *

Dew lay awake through the long, cold night, haunted by the day's tragic aftermath. Everything that could be done had been done, yet it felt like a twisted fable told around a winter fire – a distant story, but painfully real. She remembered washing her hands while someone gently took the baby from her, remembered glimpses of women bustling in and out, arranging the bodies, consoling Basil and Nettle, and then the day blurred away. In the haze, she was sure several people had tried talking to her at some point.

Now, in the darkness, she listened to Dawn's measured breathing and the wind's fierce howl outside. When she'd finally returned home, Dawn had already been asleep, blissfully unaware of what had happened. Dew tucked herself against her wife's warmth, drawn by the reassuring thrum of life in the midst of so much death. Silent tears slipped down her cheeks until exhaustion finally seized her, pulling her into a restless dream.

Basil drank. The liquor dulled the edge of grief, though never enough – never truly. He lifted another cup, swallowing hard, the burn searing his throat. Good, he thought. Pain is real. Better to feel that than face the hollow truth: two cold bodies lay downstairs, and just in the other room, a broken boy drifted into nightmares no child should know.

A man sat across from him in the dimly lit room, pouring more of whatever this fiery concoction was. Together they drank, cup after cup, until vision blurred and inhibitions fell away. In those vulnerable hours before dawn, the other man began to speak, quietly at first, then with mounting certainty about how this tragedy might have been prevented – if only they'd never turned their backs on the Factory. He spoke of medicine and machines that could sustain life, maybe even defeat death itself.

Wilder's dark hair spilled into his face, and he smiled, though there was no warmth in it. "My wife died the same way," he said. "Something as simple as a fever in the old world – yet here it means death. We live like beasts, Basil. I lost her because we have no means to save anyone."

He extended a hand across the table. "I know what you're feeling. Believe me, brother."

Basil believed him, seeing the raw hollowness beneath Wilder's show of strength. The grief, left to fester for so many years, had twisted and grown, a tumor of anger and longing. Basil knew it now – the shape of that rage. They drank again, and Wilder gazed out the window into the unrelenting storm.

"My grandfather told me of another world," Wilder said softly, his words slurring slightly from the drink. "A world without death. Let me share that with you."

Basil listened. He listened until his sorrow bled into disbelief and finally coiled itself into fury. They emptied another bottle, and by the time dawn crept through the clouds, Wilder rose and left, leaving Basil alone with the echo of his promises – and the ache of what might have been.

* * *

They held the funeral the following day.

Though the rain had weakened to a steady drizzle, a heavy pall still enveloped the valley – a lingering fog of grief and foreboding. In a meadow near the forest path that wound down to the river, the community gathered to say goodbye to a mother and child lost too soon. The sky wept with them, its tears mingling with mud and sorrow.

Ground slick and waterlogged, the pallbearers struggled to keep balance as they lowered Rosemary and her unnamed infant into a single grave. The people bowed their heads in silent reverence, each lost in a private ache. Ava stood with her parents, eyes red-rimmed. Nearby, young Nettle clutched his father's arm. Basil, rigid as stone and soaked through, refused to speak or even lift his gaze. His expression was vacant, hollow, as if some vital part of him had already followed his wife and child into the earth.

When the mound of wet soil closed over the coffin, friends and neighbors approached to share recollections of Rosemary: some bittersweet, some soft with laughter. Voice trembling, Dew recalled how the boys once flocked to Rosemary – and how she'd

battled that jealous pang until she realized she pre-
ferred girls. Fern remembered how Rosemary had
encouraged her to speak at an assembly for the first
time, while Old Maple recounted the exact moment
of her birth, even down to the curious details of the
weather. Hazel offered a gentle poem of farewell.
Others followed, spinning their own threads of
memory, until the weight of loss pressed upon
every chest.

Last to speak was Old Mossbeard, who spoke of
life's fleeting nature and the value of community. He
invited Basil to visit whenever he wished, to pour
out his sorrow, but Basil stood in numb silence, his
son clutching him for comfort he could not give.
People murmured agreement with Mossbeard's
words even as tears wet their cheeks. Further back,
in the hush beyond the crowd, stood Wilder and his
small entourage – Brook, Heather, Wolf, Aspen,
others – silent observers, their faces unreadable.

When it ended, the valley folk returned to their
homes. Fires were lit, soup prepared, garments
hung to dry. They huddled by hearths, uttering few
words and glancing at the rain outside. But at the
grave site, one figure in a dark coat lingered behind,

motionless in the shifting gloom. Basil stayed when the wind grew fierce, when the drizzle turned to hail, when lightning seared the late-afternoon sky and thunder rolled through the pines. He remained long after the valley had gone to sleep, until finally, with the day lost to the storm, he too returned to his home.

CHAPTER 8

Old Mossbeard gazed out the window at the endless rain and exhaled. How could it keep coming? He was old – very old – and had never known such a relentless downpour. Dawn had told him about the crops, about her survey with Birch. Supplies ran dangerously low. Winter would demand hunting and fishing to fill the gaps, but the wilds yielded almost nothing these days. It felt as though the sky and the community alike were fraying at the edges. Rosemary's death, and that of her baby, had struck him deeply – yet it wasn't the first time he'd seen a young mother's life cut short. The real anomaly was this bizarre storm, continuing day after day, and, of course, that other menace: the human threat from within.

He sighed and turned back to the wooden chest on his table – a muddy, half-rotten crate he'd nearly killed himself digging up just a few nights ago. Foolish risk, he thought, remembering how the flooded forest had almost claimed him. Yet somehow he'd made it back, his heart pounding with an aliveness he hadn't felt in years.

The chest was large and rectangular, its curved lid bound by iron fittings that had rusted but held firm. Dirt clung to every crevice, and it looked as though it might crumble at the gentlest touch. Like me, he mused with a grim smile. Carefully, he lifted the lid, hands trembling. Inside, in two neat rows, lay twenty hammers. He recognized them intimately: the weight of iron in his grip, the rush of power, the sense of unstoppable possibility – and the gruesome impact once the hammer fell.

He picked one up – his own. The head looked like ruddy copper, though it was iron. The handle was worn from years past. At its base, the word he'd etched long ago still showed: Remember. He did remember, all too clearly.

Pascal's hammer thrust toward the Tower.

"We have nothing to lose but our chains!"

He felt the swell of unity back then, a faceless figure among gray-uniformed soldiers, all raised fists and roaring chants, the Tower rocking on its foundations.

Pascal's trembling voice:

"No one is free – not a single one of us – until all are free!"

The machines, the pounding roar, and Mars – emerging from the pyre – lifting her own hammer high. Then came the blood...

Shuddering, Mossbeard placed another log on the fire. These hammers shouldn't exist, he told himself. They'd abandoned them with the Factory, or so the story went. But he'd sneaked some out, and others had, too, as if they had never truly committed to leaving the old world behind. Had they simply pretended? he wondered, thinking of those who had worn the revolution's colors but never fully embraced it – those who had shifted sides when they'd seen the profit in it. Some of his fellow grays; Hammer's closest followers, such as Wilder's grandfather.

He remembered how fervently he'd believed in the revolution, how he'd given everything he had, looking for redemption, yet he'd stashed away these hammers for decades, silent. Perhaps, he thought, I'm just another uniform. He no longer recalled being a worker, not truly. Soldiers were chosen from among them, but based on what criteria? What was it in him that had compelled them to turn him into a gray? Did the revolution's downfall start the day they handed hammers to men like him? Maybe, he muttered inwardly, we soldiers should have perished with the Tower.

He flexed his fingers around the hammer's handle, listening to the drum of rain on the roof. He should never have grown old, he told himself. But here he was. Now, someone needed to know about these hammers – someone who could wield them for true freedom, the very purpose Pascal had given them. Because Remember was more than a word scrawled on iron – it was a warning, a call to action he could no longer ignore.

* * *

The sun, such as it was, dipped behind the valley's rim, though no one could really tell beneath the oppressive clouds. Rain alternated with bouts of small, stinging hail, and gusts of wind roamed the village lanes, rattling shutters and peeling away the last scraps of warmth. The river, now twice its usual width, churned with violent force. Fish were gone, game nowhere to be found, crops drowned beyond saving. An unkind autumn, indeed.

Yet inside Hazel's home, a soft glow still promised comfort. Fires crackled from dawn till dusk, banishing the gray chill outside. The kitchen gave off the scent of bread and potatoes, a reminder that life continued despite looming scarcity. Hazel's parents worked in near-silence – tending the fire, preparing supper, patching small repairs – while the younger crowd played cards in the front room. Nettle was among them, though he spoke little since the day his mother and unborn sister had been laid to rest.

Occasionally, Hazel noticed tears welling in the boy's eyes. "It's alright," she would murmur, placing a gentle hand on his shoulder. "We're here, Nettle." Ava, seated beside her, would whisper 'Give him space' or 'Let him heal in his own time,' and Janis would nod affirmatively before turning his attention back to the game.

They played Streams and Rivers, a simple card game beloved by the valley folk. Enough of a challenge to stay interesting, but easy enough to follow without heavy strategizing. Janis, liberated from chores for once, took it quite seriously. He mentioned how Iris – despite her aversion to seasonings and the resulting rivalry she held with Ava's mother – had kindly volunteered to check on his sick mother that evening, leaving him free to relax.

"Boo-ya!" Janis boasted, slamming down his final card and nearly jumping from his seat. "I've crushed your puny streams with my mighty river!" He turned to Ava, waggling his eyebrows. "Have you ever witnessed such a glorious river, Ava? Have you?"

Hazel shot him a warning glance, nodding toward Nettle, whose expression remained blank. Janis's grin wavered. "Ah – right. Uh... good game, Nettle. Your, er, stream was a real threat there for a moment."

Hazel's father caught the exchange from the kitchen. "Is he always like this?" he asked with an amused sigh.

"Absolutely," Ava and Hazel answered in unison, prompting Nettle's lips to curl in a fleeting smile.

They played a few more rounds. Gradually, Nettle loosened up, drawn in by Janis's antics – perhaps precisely because Janis treated him no differently than before. The boy even confided the name of his stuffed donkey: "Donkey," crafted from real donkey hair by his mother. Hazel noticed the soft glow returning to his eyes. She forced a laugh at Janis's terrible jokes; Ava tried her own humor but slipped, accidentally bringing Nettle to tears. Hazel kicked her lightly under the table and murmured for her to hush.

Before supper could be served, angry knocking pounded against the door. Hazel's parents exchanged uneasy looks as her father went to open it, revealing Basil – tall, grim, drenched in rain, face hardened by an unspoken anger.

"Nettle," he said, not sparing any courtesy. "I need you to come with me."

Hazel's father offered help. Basil shook him off and walked straight into the house, tramping mud on the floor, grasping Nettle's hand in silence.

"Basil?" Hazel's mother ventured softly, her voice uncertain. "Please... stay for dinner? You must be cold."

"No." He barely looked at her. "I'm just here for my son."

Nettle's eyes darted between the adults, searching for reassurance. Basil gave none, leading the boy out into the dark. The door slammed, leaving Hazel's parents pale with shock, Ava and Hazel speechless, and the little donkey toy forgotten on the table.

Janis, scratching his head, broke the silence. "That was... weird. So, uh–another round of Streams and Rivers, anyone?"

* * *

Nightfall settled over the valley as a weary hush. The storm's fury hadn't let up – rain mingled with ragged bouts of hail, and the wind howled through every gap in the doors and windows. Inside, Dew and Dawn sat at the counter, teacups in hand, letting the silence do most of the talking.

Over the years, words between them had lost some of their urgency. Now they served only to grant shape and edge to what both already knew.

Dawn let her fingers trace gentle patterns across Dew's palm. "Hey," she said. "You alright?"

"Not really. Sorry," Dew admitted.

"I know you still blame yourself," Dawn said, thinking of Rosemary's and her child's death, which lingered in every unspoken corner of their days. Time had passed, but the wound remained fresh.

Dew tried to deny it, but her shoulders sagged. "You're right. I do."

"There's nothing you could have done differently, love. We've dissected it a thousand times."

Dew inhaled slowly, cradling her teacup in both hands. "I know. But it doesn't stop the feeling."

Outside, rain battered the walls, and Dawn felt Dew's sorrow roll through the room like a cold draft. They shared each other's burdens as surely as they shared warmth. And death, it seemed, was not through haunting the valley. May, Janis's mother, grew weaker by the day. Who would be next?

"What are we going to do?" Dew asked, meeting Dawn's eyes. "We'll never make it to spring with the supplies we have. There's just no way."

Dawn sighed and placed her hands over Dew's, squeezing gently. "I'm not sure. But we'll figure it out somehow." She tried for a smile. "Maybe we'll find enough game and fish after all. Maybe the stores will hold up better than we expect. We can't leave, that's for sure. The mountains offer no refuge."

She stood, sliding her arms around Dew and pressing a kiss to her neck. The small jolt of intimacy almost kept the worry at bay.

Glancing out the window, Dew noticed a figure trudging through the mud, laboring up the hill. "We have a visitor," she said, frowning. "Looks like Aspen."

Dew opened the door, letting in a blast of frigid air and the boy's slumped form. Mud caked his boots; rainwater dripped from his hood. She guided him to the fire, handed him a blanket, and poured another steaming cup of tea.

"Thanks," he managed through chattering teeth.

"Of course," Dew said.

"What brings you?" Dawn asked, never one for small talk. She realized with a start she hadn't seen the boy since the funeral, though the whole valley spoke of him and his parents – and all the other members of Wilder's group.

"A message," Aspen said, sipping tea more leisurely than the situation deserved. "From Wilder."

Dew exchanged a look with Dawn. "Why didn't he come himself?"

"He's... busy," Aspen answered. "A lot of us are helping him."

"Helping with what?" Dew pressed, voice skeptical.

Aspen took his time, letting the silence stretch. Dawn's fingers drummed impatiently on the counter.

"You'll find out at the emergency assembly," he said at last.

"Emergency assembly?" Dawn repeated, her tone going sharp.

"Day after tomorrow, noon, at the tavern, as usual." Aspen shrugged. "I'm supposed to inform everyone." He glanced at his teacup. "Good tea, by the way. Chamomile?"

Dawn's eyebrows shot up. "What kind of emergency, exactly?"

He gestured to the window. "Just look outside. Crops failing, storms never-ending –"

"We held an assembly about that two weeks ago," Dawn cut in. "But neither you nor Wilder bothered to show."

Aspen stiffened. "That meeting was illegitimate. We need a real assembly. One with actual solutions."

Dawn bristled, standing. "What's that supposed to mean?"

"Hey," Aspen said, raising a hand. "Don't shoot the messenger."

Dew touched Dawn's arm, signaling her to calm down. "Alright," she said to Aspen. "Day after tomorrow at noon. Got it."

Relief flickered across Aspen's face. "So you'll come?"

"Wouldn't want it to be illegitimate, right?" Dawn retorted, eyes glinting.

Aspen forced a thin smile, something cold gleaming behind it. "Good one."

"Where's Wilder been all this time?" Dew asked. "We haven't seen him since the funeral."

"I don't know," Aspen said. "Barely seen him myself lately."

Dawn snorted her disbelief. Aspen finished his tea with a noisy gulp.

"Anyway," he said, standing up, "I'd better go. More people to inform. Thanks for the tea."

"Be careful out there," Dew told him as another flash of lightning lit the window.

"It's just weather," Aspen said, feigning a casual shrug.

He pulled his coat tight, jammed his muddied boots on, and disappeared into the twilight. Dew and Dawn watched him wade through the swirling gusts and thought the same silent thought: something is coming.

Later that evening, Old Mossbeard poked at the embers in his tiny hearth, a faded robe draped around his stooped frame. He wore an eccentric shirt patterned with colorful flowers that looked almost alive in the flickering firelight.

"Another assembly, hmm?" he echoed, glancing up at Aspen. The boy looked drained; it was late, and Mossbeard had heard Aspen pounding for a good ten minutes before letting him in.

Aspen nodded. "Yes. Day after tomorrow, at noon."

"And called by Wilder?" The old man nudged a log with his staff. His loose trousers sagged on his thin hips, revealing far more than Aspen cared to see. He quickly averted his gaze.

"That's right," Aspen said, focusing on the floor.

Mossbeard settled on a stool beside him, creaking with every move. "Something else you're not telling me, boy?"

"What do you mean?"

The old man's cloudy eyes seemed to pierce right through him. "Just a feeling," he murmured. "You seem... tense."

"It's the weather," Aspen said, wiping a bead of sweat from his brow. "And I'm tired."

"Tired, eh? Couldn't you have come by tomorrow?"

Aspen shook his head. "Too many duties tomorrow, all for the assembly. Sorry."

Mossbeard nodded, turning back to the fire. "All very mysterious. A mysterious assembly, called by a mysterious man." He looked over his shoulder at Aspen. "You want to know what I think?"

Aspen swallowed. "Sure."

"You –" Mossbeard paused, letting the tension build. Aspen braced himself, half expecting an accusation.

"You need to eat something, boy!"

Aspen exhaled in relief.

"Look at you – skin and bones!" Mossbeard said. "Don't your folks feed you?"

Aspen tried to smile, noting the old man's trembling shuffle. He'd aged fast these past years, and even his once-impressive beard seemed sparser. But it still harbored tangles of moss...and was that a spider?

"I'll fetch you some food," Mossbeard offered. He waddled toward the kitchen, coughing lightly. Aspen gazed out the window, missing the storm's cold clarity over this awkward scene. The old man took that moment to slide the chest behind a cluttered shelf, stacking crates and baskets to hide it from view.

"Can I help?" Aspen called.

"No, no, sit tight," Mossbeard replied. He pulled out some stale bread and cheese, rearranging more supplies to cloak the chest. Satisfied it was hidden, he returned with the meager meal.

Aspen whistled softly, nibbling on the bread.

Mossbeard thought of the hammers in that chest – of how he needed to stash them somewhere safer. He'd unearthed them on a fool's impulse, nearly losing his life in the process without anyone knowing where he'd gone. Anyway, it was too soon to bring them up. Not until he saw what Wilder's assembly would reveal. Violence would be the very last resort. If necessary, he'd inform Dawn. Let her decide.

I'm too old to fight, Mossbeard told himself as he passed Aspen his supper, feigning nonchalance. Too worn out to rehash old battles.

When Aspen finished eating, he left without ceremony, and Mossbeard stared at the embers in the silence of his hut. The night was cold, his memories colder still. At last, he curled up in a restless sleep, uncertain what the next dawn would bring.

CHAPTER 9

The road was narrow and slick with mud, made worse by the relentless rain – if such a thing as a dry day existed anymore, no one in the valley remembered it. The old autumn had vanished abruptly, ceding power to an early winter creeping in from the edges of the forest. Winds slashed through the branches with an icy bite, leaving Ava and Hazel clutching each other's hands for warmth and balance. Their boots sank into the mire as they trudged onward, hooded figures in a world dissolving under clouds.

Hazel cast a glance at Ava. "You think Aspen will be there?"

Ava sighed, wishing she could avoid this topic. "Yes. Everyone will be there."

"Right." Hazel tugged her coat tighter, cheeks half-hidden by the collar. "You think he'll, um... notice me?"

Ava halted, letting out an exasperated groan. She squeezed Hazel's hand until she squeaked. "Hazel, for the last time, he's not interested. You deserve better than that jerk."

"Okay, okay!" Hazel raised her free hand. "Sorry for asking."

They continued through the mud in brooding silence. A distant dog barked, and wind barreled through bare-limbed trees, eerily vacant of leaves. Hazel peered sidelong at Ava.

Ava groaned again. "You're still thinking about him."

Hazel shrugged. "I can't help it. And what other boys are there? You name one."

"Martens?" suggested Ava, half-joking.

"Ugh, he's too old. And weird."

"All right, fine," Ava said. "What about Janis?"

Hazel laughed. "Janis is like a brother. Trust me, that'd be a disaster."

Ava managed a lopsided grin. "Then at least promise me: no more pies."

Hazel lifted her hands in mock surrender. "No more pies, I swear. Not in a hundred years. Besides, we're out of raspberries."

Ahead of them loomed the tavern now, a two-story relic of rotting timbers and cold stone. Overgrown evergreen shrubs crowded around it like bored sentinels. Ava recalled stories of how this place had once been buzzing with travelers and ambassadors from other communities, back when times had been less desperate. These days, it served mostly for drinking, card games, and the increasingly rare community gathering. No point in beautifying a building no one much cared about.

A dull glow leaked from shuttered windows. "I think we're late," Ava said.

"Probably," Hazel agreed. "I just hope it's warm inside." She led the way, pushing through a thicket that had taken over the path. Then she froze, hearing muffled shouts from within. "What's going on?"

"I've never heard Dawn like that," Ava murmured, tension rising in her voice.

They exchanged uneasy looks. Retreat was possible – someone would fill them in later. But it was too cold out here, and the thought of a warming fire and some hot tea was irresistible.

"All right," Ava said. She grabbed the handle and pulled open the door.

From a small rise overlooking the tavern, a figure watched in silence, her arms folded across her chest. Ren, exhausted from weeks of trudging through rain and highland paths, was caked in mud and smelled of desperation. She'd arrived in the valley two days ago, silently observing until she knew what she was dealing with, only to find that everything was worse than she'd imagined. The storm wasn't quite as catastrophic as predicted – but it would last way longer. Now she stood, trembling with fatigue.

Two men hovered a few steps from the tavern's entrance, having arrived right after Ava and Hazel disappeared inside. They seemed to be guarding the entrance. Through the slanting rain, Ren observed one of them shift – and the faint glint of metal caught her eye.

A rifle? Her heart jumped, and she ducked behind a tree, creeping closer through the wind-battered firs until their hushed words reached her.

"Just keep it together," said the taller one.

Ren recognized him: Basil. He'd changed since she'd last seen him – shoulders broader, beard thicker, and an aura of pent-up rage. Not like him at all.

"We've practiced," Basil continued. "We'll be fine."

The other man nodded, gaze darting about nervously. Brook, Ren realized. Heather's husband. She vaguely recalled their son – Aspen was his name. Brook's eyes slid around, as if seeking an escape.

"I'm just saying," he mumbled. "Are we absolutely sure about this? I mean –"

"Are you serious?" Basil snapped. His voice rose, temper already fraying. "You said you'd follow Wilder anywhere. You said we'd all die if we didn't do this – that the valley depends on us."

Brook swallowed. "I did, yes. And I do trust him, but maybe there's another way?"

"What way?!" Basil's fury flared, the stench of alcohol rolling off him. "My wife bled to death because this place has nothing – no knowledge, no technology, no medicine. Nothing!"

Brook shrank a step back. "I'm sorry... I just –"

"Don't be. Don't say you're fucking sorry." Basil cradled his rifle like a lover. "We have to make them see, and Wilder's the only one who can lead us. He's studied the past like no one else. He's dedicated his life to this. There's no one else."

Brook sat on a nearby boulder, shoulders slumped. "You're right. Just wish it didn't have to be like this. They'll hate us. For them, we will be the bad guys."

"It's for the best," Basil insisted, voice eerily calm. "Better than letting them bury more mothers. More children." There was a longing in the man's eyes. "Did Wilder ever tell you about doctors? Real doctors, I mean. And hospitals? Every civilization had hospitals."

"Yeah, he mentioned it," said Brook.

Basil smiled. "You know, my wife could be alive right now. My daughter could be alive."

"Yes."

"But they're both dead."

"So they are."

From her vantage, Ren felt a chill that went beyond the storm. She recognized this brand of madness – a darkness she'd hoped was gone for good. Then Basil pressed his ear to the tavern door, grinning at the uproar within.

"Sounds like it's starting. You ready?" Basil asked, eyes wild.

Brook nodded, reluctant. "Ready."

A sudden shot cracked inside, splitting the tempest's roar. A heartbeat of absolute stillness followed, then a sickening thud. Ren's stomach clenched. It's all happening again, she thought. Screams surged from inside, raw and terrified.

The two men locked eyes, checked their rifles – Brook's hands trembled on the bolt – then Basil kicked in the door. Ren, hidden in the dripping branches, could do nothing as the scene descended into chaos.

Far in the distance, an eagle soared over snow-capped peaks. It twisted with predatory grace, letting out a piercing cry as it circled invisible thermal currents. Spying movement below, it dove with lethal speed. The prey was unsuspecting, believing itself secure. The bird struck in a flurry of talons and feathers, tearing flesh, devouring what little life was left in the rabbit.

Safety was an illusion, stability a trap. The storm raged, the rifles roared, and dreams vanished under the shadow of wings.

* * *

Janis and his mother stared at each other across the cramped upstairs bedroom, where a single candle flickered. She was propped against a threadbare pillow, too weak to leave her bed. He sat on a hard wooden chair, ladling a dubious broth he'd made earlier. Everyone else was at the assembly – out in that cursed weather – so caring for May fell to him alone.

"Come on, Mum," he coaxed, bringing the spoon close to her lips. "Just a few more bites."

He tried his usual antics: mimicking bird calls and swooping the spoon in an absurd arc, eyebrows dancing in cartoonish ways. A dribble of soup landed on the blankets.

"Careful!" May scolded, breaking into a frail laugh that soon gave way to coughing. "Sounds like a robin. Who taught you that?"

"No one." He gave a half-smile. "Taught myself. It's not so hard."

"Smart boy," she said, then dissolved into another fit of coughs. Janis waited it out before easing another spoonful past her lips.

"You don't have to hover over me all day," she managed, between slow breaths.

He shrugged. "I want to."

"I'm sure your friends miss you."

Janis smirked. "Oh, they're lost without me. But I'd rather be here."

She didn't argue, so he scooped another spoonful. After swallowing, her gaze grew serious. "I won't be around much longer, Janis." Her tone was calm, almost resigned.

He paused mid-ladle, eyes on the swirling broth. "I know."

Shifting against the pillows, she tried to sit upright. "Why not let someone else help tomorrow? You can take some time off."

He sidestepped the suggestion. "We'll see. The weather's shit anyway, so might as well torment you."

"You're not tormenting me, you know."

"Yeah, yeah."

"I'm serious."

He just shrugged. "Sure, Mum."

She exhaled slowly. "You're just like your father, you know?"

"Dead?" He said it impulsively, feeling a tiny stab of regret at his grim humor.

May almost choked, then laughed until it hurt. "Oh yes. Exactly like him – always some snarky line at the worst moment." Her face contorted with pain. "And a kind heart behind it all."

He softened. "If you say so."

A rumble of thunder rattled the rafters. The room was too cold, but May had refused to move downstairs to the fireplace, insisting she didn't want to alarm her son's friends with her sight. Janis had given up arguing.

"That's why the girls like you, you know," May said, her voice still ragged.

Janis groaned. "You realize how 'Mum' that sounds?"

"But it's true! Don't Ava and Hazel hang around you all the time? And what about that other girl? The one –"

"They're just friends, Mum. You know that."

She pressed on, ignoring his protest. "You really are just like your father – never noticing when someone likes you, even if she were to dance in her undies right in front of you!"

"Oh, come on!" He covered his face. "I'm trying to feed you here!"

"It's true." She coughed again, weaker now.

Janis summoned a smirk. "Trust me, I'd notice if Ava or Hazel were dancing around in their underwear."

"Uh-huh."

He gritted his teeth and slid the last spoonful of broth into her mouth. She swallowed, and he sighed with relief. An entire bowl done, and no big mess.

"Well, what about Aspen?" she ventured, as he dabbed at her mouth with a cloth. "He's a handsome boy, isn't he?"

Janis groaned. "Mum, I like girls, remember?"

She grinned mischievously. "I swear he was looking at you at the solstice festival –"

"That was months ago!" Janis nearly shot up from his chair. "He danced with six different girls that night. Six."

"He's probably overcompensating. His parents are no good." She paused. "Maybe you should give it some thought –"

"No, Mum!"

She chuckled, then grimaced at the ache it triggered. "Fine. Calm down." She flopped back against the pillows, feigning offense. "Imagine, yelling at your dying mother. I should've raised you with more manners..."

He rolled his eyes and counted to ten. "Yeah, well..." Janis began, but then a deafening crack tore through the air, reverberating like thunder. The world seemed to freeze. This was no thunder, Janis thought. He jolted to his feet.

"What the hell was that?" he muttered.

May's eyes were wide. "It must have come from the assembly."

He rushed to the window but could see only a blurry sheet of rain. May forced her voice steadier than she felt. "Put out the fire and the candles, Janis – now!"

He whirled around. "Why?"

"Just do it, please," she insisted, a raw urgency in her eyes. "I don't like this."

He moved without further argument, hurrying downstairs. As he went, May's words echoed in his mind. She's scared. And if she was scared, then something truly awful must be happening.

CHAPTER 10

Wilder stood on the makeshift platform they'd constructed over the past few days. Simple pictograms and carvings adorned it – predators hunting prey, half-finished silhouettes of curious towers – all melded into some sort of statement. On the front, Heather had painted a large, blood-red eagle, talons braced for the kill. Four men had carried the platform into place; it groaned faintly under its own weight.

Inside the tavern, tension gripped the crowd like a vise, an undercurrent of outrage and fear. Here and there, people shouted, but mostly they stared at Wilder, who loomed atop the platform with dark hair plastered to his face. Time itself seemed to hold its breath – later, they'd claim they remembered every detail of this day, as if the moments had etched themselves into collective memory.

"And whose fault is that?" Wilder demanded, glaring down at Dawn.

"No one's, you fool!" Dawn fired back, greeted by scattered cheers. "We can't control storms or –"

"The storm," he sneered. "The weather, the rains, the crops – excuses, all of it! Where are your solutions, Dawn?"

"Solutions?" she sputtered. "What are you suggesting –?"

He slammed a fist into the air. "We'll starve!" He swept his gaze over the crowd, locking eyes with each stunned face. "We'll all die because you – and the chaos you represent – have failed!" A roar of agreement rose from the first row, where Moose – bald and bellowing – led the clamor. By his side hovered Wolf, Heather, Aspen, Old Cedar, and several others.

"We're not lords and ladies of the earth," Birch interjected, stepping to Dawn's side. His cheeks flamed red, and his mustache twitched with indignation. "If we failed, then we failed together – those on the fields and orchards, on the riverbanks, in the forests. It's on all of us!" He leveled a trembling finger at Wilder. "And we'll survive, the way we always did!"

Dawn raised her voice so all could hear. "Wilder – where were you all this time? Why didn't you help? I haven't seen you lift a finger. Where the hell were you?"

Insults and accusations burst from every corner. Those up front whipped around, shouting for the rest to shut up. Wilder froze, momentarily unsure. Meanwhile, Dew tried to calm Dawn, who ignored her. In the back, Ava and Hazel slipped in, pale with confusion. They clung to each other, minds spinning. Mossbeard spotted them and beckoned them closer.

"Mossbeard!" Ava gasped. "What's happening?"

The old man just shook his head gravely, gesturing for them to sit. Old Maple tried to reassure them – "It's just an argument" – but Ava and Hazel, seeing the fury blazing in every face, doubted her words.

Near the side of the platform, Heather leaned in to whisper in Wilder's ear. "Everything's fine," he told her, though his face was taut with worry. This was not going as planned. He'd boasted that they'd "fall in line like sheep," too frightened to refuse a strong leader. Wrong, she thought grimly. They're furious.

When the first arrivals had seen the platform, they'd been perplexed by its ominous symbols. Wilder had only smiled and said, "Wait and see." The seating arrangement – rows instead of the usual circles – had raised hackles too, especially when Wilder's followers claimed the front seats, effectively shutting out those who tried to speak. Anyone who tried approaching the stage was turned away by Wolf or Heather. Those who came later simply followed the pattern, sitting in uneasy silence.

Finally, Wilder murmured something to Wolf, who unleashed a roar powerful enough to halt an entire wolf pack. A hush fell; all eyes returned to the platform. Wilder, adopting a look of calm composure, spread his arms.

"You see this, my friends? This is chaos. This is decay. This is how we die." He motioned to Dawn, then Birch, River, and others. "I've had enough. Enough incompetence and excuses –"

"I'm not listening to this lunacy!" Birch declared, stomping toward Wolf and trying to shoulder past. Wolf braced himself, a wall of muscle, and they exchanged words no one else could hear.

No one was prepared for the blow to Birch's temple. The cracking sound echoed throughout the tavern. A single gasp of horror rippled through the throng as Birch toppled, limbs slack as a discarded puppet. His skull struck the wooden boards with a second, sickening thud, eyes wide, unblinking.

A collective heartbeat of paralyzed stillness. Wilder gaped, Wolf stared at his own fist, the crowd tensed like a single muscle. Then all at once, the gathering erupted in rage and terror – parents shielding children, people lurching to their feet, fists raised. Dawn grabbed Dew's hand, desperate to find safety, but there was none. The throng surged, chairs overturned, screams tangled with curses. Those loyal to Wilder were overwhelmed, pressed back like reeds in a flood.

Heather, Wolf, and a handful of supporters retreated to the platform steps, shielding Wilder. He watched the chaos with an uncanny grin. Far to one side, River hurled himself at Wolf, nearly felling the giant. Wolf stumbled but caught his balance. Heather and Aspen flattened themselves against a wall, eyes full of alarm. From her vantage, Dawn saw a glint of metal in Wilder's arms.

"Is that...?" she whispered.

"No," Dew gasped. "Please, no."

Mossbeard struggled to guide Ava, Hazel, and Old Maple toward the exit. This is the moment for the hammers, he thought in despair, but I hid them away like a fool. The madness boiled at the platform's base: Wilder's men had lost control, battered by the furious crowd. Then Wilder lifted his weapon – an unmistakable rifle, gleaming with lethal promise.

The shot thundered through the tavern, and the entire crowd froze. Splinters rained from the rafters where the bullet tore a path. The acrid smell of powder joined the reek of Birch's blood. Ava and Hazel clutched their ears, tears streaking their faces, panic throbbing in every pulse.

An instant later, the door slammed open. Two more men burst in, rifles leveled. Basil and Brook. A hush descended as people cowered, goosebumps flaring at the sight of so much firepower. Wilder lowered his rifle, letting a grin crawl across his lips.

"No more!" Wilder roared. "No more chaos! No more useless assemblies, no more bickering!" He gestured to the red eagle painted on the platform. Beside it, Birch's corpse lay sprawled, blood creeping across the boards. "A new era starts now. We are in control."

His eyes raked the crowd, calculating who might still resist. Determined to make another example, he signaled Wolf and Basil. "Bring me River," he growled.

A muted groan swept the tavern. Wolf and Basil stomped forward, aiming their rifles. The masses parted. Fern clung to her husband, trembling, but River stood motionless, either in shock or acceptance. Mossbeard, from the back, yelled, "No! Don't let them – they'll kill him!"

"Shut up!" Wilder spun, rifle aimed at the old man. "Not another word!"

Mossbeard choked on his pleas. "Wilder, please... end this madness –"

"Quiet!" Another shot slammed the rafters, wood fragments tumbling down. Wilder swung the barrel toward Dawn, who flinched. Dew shielded her, eyes frantic. "All of you shut up, or the next bullet's for her," Wilder hissed.

Ava darted forward, trying to reach her father as Wolf and Basil hauled him onto the platform. She pounded Wolf's back. "Stop! Let him go!"

Wolf jerked around, but Dew seized Ava, pulling her away. Wolf would kill her without hesitation, she thought. The dam's broken. "It's all right," River croaked, his voice shaky. "It'll be all right."

He was forced to his knees. Wilder offered the crowd a mocking shrug. "I want you to learn something very important," he said. "And I won't repeat it."

He inhaled sharply. "The times of chaos are over!" He flipped his rifle butt-first and rammed it into River's gut. River went down, gasping for breath. Fern screamed, collapsing beside Ava. Wilder landed another vicious kick to River's ribs, and something inside him gave with a sickening crack.

Hazel crouched with Ava and Fern, trying to block the sight. Dew hovered near Dawn, terrified. Around them, Wilder's men grabbed rifles from wooden crates – some held their weapons in obvious shock, others stood proud. Wolf and Basil towered above River's agony, rifles trained on the crowd. Birch's blood dripped from the platform.

Breathing heavily, Wilder pinned them all with a measured gaze. "I know this is hard to accept, but trust me: everything changes now." He threw his arms wide, almost a performance. "My friends, my family – this is for you. We can build something better if we stand united. For us, for the children – look at them!" He nodded at a child sobbing in the corner, then carried on, ignoring River's ragged cough. "I know you're wondering where I've been. I was at the Factory, and I bring troubling news. It's not what they told you it was –" He jabbed a finger at Mossbeard, who knelt, head bowed in despair. "It's not a place of oppression. It's glorious – machines, structures, efficiency! They lied to us, and they will answer for it."

Eyes flicked from one to another in numb disbelief. The uproar had become a stunned hush. Dawn stood with the others, heart hammering, baffled at how so many listened to this madness. Wilder ranted on about "order and progress," about how they would all live under the Eagles' watchful eyes now – no tyranny, he insisted, just parental guidance, an end to starvation and chaos.

He nodded at Brook, who brandished his rifle in the air. "Long live the valley! Long live the Eagles! Long live Wilder!" the loyalists roared. The rest stayed silent, dazed by the violence. Fern and Ava sobbed over River's motionless form now, while Birch's blood still seeped into the floor.

Dawn forced herself forward. Enough. Let them kill me if they want. She stepped onto the platform's edge. Wilder noticed her approach, eyes narrowing.

"Have you lost your mind?" Dawn spat. "Did someone bash out your last scrap of reason?"

"Dawn, no!" Dew lunged for her, but Dawn shook free. "You maniac," Dawn snarled. "I'm glad your wife isn't here to see what a monster you've become."

Aspen clubbed her from the side with his rifle. The impact made a dull crack that echoed in the hush. She collapsed backward into Dew's arms.

"No!" Dew screamed, cradling Dawn's limp body. Aspen smirked, seeking approval. Wilder's expression twitched with anger – this hadn't been part of the plan. They must not turn Dawn into a martyr. Not her. The crowd recoiled, some crying, some cursing. Mossbeard moaned in horror.

Wilder steadied himself. "Take her to the prison," he ordered softly, motioning to the men around him. "And River, too." The man on the floor convulsed in shallow breaths. "Let Dew tend to them – stop the bleeding and keep them alive. For now." He glared over at Ava, who was sobbing in Hazel's arms, blocked from following her father. Heather and Brook hefted Dawn's limp body; two others dragged River's. Slowly they retreated through the door, while the rest of Wilder's group aimed rifles at the crowd, keeping them at bay.

Turning back to the rest, Wilder exhaled. "I regret this. Truly. Let it be known that they'll receive care. But from this day, any disobedience will be punished." He paused, letting that sink in. "Go home. Think it over. Tomorrow, we begin anew. The Eagles guard the valley, so do not leave your houses without permission. If you're caught outside –" He raised his rifle. "You'll die."

He waited, daring anyone to protest. No one spoke. He stepped down from the platform, whispered instructions to Moose and a few others, then strode out, Wolf and Basil at his side, ignoring Mossbeard's pleading. Aspen followed close behind, chest puffed with a twisted pride.

The people stood trembling, tears flooding the corners of their vision. Blood dripped from the stage, plopped onto the tavern floor. Birch lay stiff, dead as stone, with Eagles guarding the body. Wilder's remaining men emptied the tavern. No conversation, no comfort. Hazel and her family led Fern and Ava back home. Mossbeard limped out, rejecting all help.

The Eagles, under Moose's direction, hauled Birch's body into the forest, digging a shallow grave in the mud. Then some left to begin their patrol, while the rest drifted to Wilder's house. They had much to plan. Their new order had only begun, and the future, as they saw it, belonged to them.

Rain battered the valley through the day and into the deep hours of night, soaking fields and forests without mercy. The air was a blade of ice, and fires did little to fend off the damp chill. Families gathered around flickering hearths but felt strangely alone, as though each flame burned in its own sealed bubble. They coaxed dogs inside, coaxed cats that would follow – any living warmth to stave off the black night.

Still, a grim presence loomed in the storm's howl and the rifle's echo, in the drowned meadows and the flooding river, most of all in the dark forests. A hush lay over them, a hush that was not peace but oppression, a hush that signaled a cage had descended – no walls, no bars, yet unbreakable. For the first time in living memory, freedom had slipped away, swallowed by the shadow of new masters.

EPILOGUE

"Unconscious?"

"Yes – and Dew's with her. A few others, too. I can't see who. They're carrying someone else. A man, I think." Janis panted, his breath uneven. He was sweating. "Mom, Dawn's bleeding. She looks –"

"Don't let them see you!" May rasped, every cough rattling her frail body.

Janis crouched by the window, heart pounding at the procession emerging from the tavern. Minutes earlier, those terrifying booms – then figures in gray moving about with strange, heavy contraptions in their hands. Rifles, his mother had said. Deadly weapons from the Factory.

"Where are they going, Janis?" May asked.

"I – I'm not sure... The forest, I think." His eyes darted to her, voice trembling. "Mom, what did they do to Dawn? What's happening out there?"

May let out a long, wheezing sigh. "I don't know."

"But those bangs –"

"Gunshots," she murmured. "Mossbeard said rifles can kill in an instant."

Janis swallowed hard. "Kill people? This was just supposed to be a boring assembly – how could it –"

"I know as little as you, dear," May said, coughing again. He pressed a cup of water to her lips. Then, another glimpse through the window:

"Mom, there's someone else coming."

"Don't let them see you," she hissed again.

He peered outside, frowning. "It's... weird," he whispered. "Their arms – legs – they're moving so strangely." The figure flitted behind houses, reappearing in half-seen flashes. Finally, it huddled behind a tree, leaning into the faint twilight. Janis gasped. "Mom, it's Ren!"

"Ren?" May echoed, half-incredulous. "No one's seen her in ages."

"Yeah, it's her!" In his excitement, Janis threw open the window despite May's protest. Rain lashed his face. "Ren! We're here!"

The figure snapped up, alarmed. Then, with a fleeting twitch of her thin mouth, she signaled toward the back door. Moments later, she vanished from sight.

"Janis, wait –" May began, but he was already bounding downstairs.

He yanked the door open, letting in a gust of freezing air. Ren slipped inside, drenched and shivering, the sharp odor of soaked leather and sweat clinging to her. She lifted her hood, revealing the tired, delicate features Janis still remembered.

"Hello, Janis." Her eyes lingered on him, as though recalling an old friend. "You've grown."

He let out a strangled laugh. "Vegetables," he said hastily, then sobered. "Ren... what the hell is going on out there?!"

"Keep your voice down," she snapped, scanning the shadows. "Wilder and his men – 'the Eagles,' they call themselves – are seizing control. Is your mother here?"

Janis nodded. "Upstairs. She's ill."

Ren brushed past him, heading for the stairs two at a time. "We don't have much time."

Upstairs, May struggled upright at the sound of footsteps. When Ren entered, May's tension eased into a smile. "Ren! It really is you." But her relief dissolved into alarm. "What happened at the tavern? Shots – people –"

"Wilder's group," Ren said, glancing out the window. "They've taken over. They killed Birch. I think Dawn and River are in custody – alive, I hope. It's too dangerous to stay. We have to go."

"Go?" May echoed, her voice unsteady. She filed away Birch's death for later. "Ren, look at me." She gestured to her wasted frame under the blankets.

Ren peeled the cover back, biting her lip at the sight of May's frail body. "The cancer's worse," she said quietly.

"Yes. I can't go anywhere," May whispered.

Janis hovered in the doorway, cheeks gone pale. Ren pulled up May's blanket and turned to him.

"They're forming a prison, Janis. Birch is dead, and others may follow. Wilder's men have rifles, and the rest of the valley is trapped. We must leave – tonight."

Janis watched his mother, his throat tight. May forced a smile. "Janis, you have to go. You can't stay."

"No!" he blurted, kneeling by her side, tears stinging. "Mum, I won't leave you here, not like this."

She cupped his cheek. "Listen to me. If you stay, you'll starve – or worse, die at Wilder's hands. You have to go with Ren."

Ren nodded, softly. "I'll take care of him."

Janis felt as though his chest might split. "Mum, I..."

May mustered a small, trembling smile. 'I'll still be here, dear. I'm no danger to them. The others can look after me, and maybe I'll get better. When spring comes, we'll fish again, just you and me."

He wanted to believe it. But part of him knew otherwise.

* *

Ren left them briefly to gather supplies: Janis's clothes, food from the basement, anything portable and warm. She planned their route in her head – through the forest, across the mountains, all under endless storm clouds. Even if Wilder's men didn't bother chasing them, traveling would be slow with a boy who'd never journeyed far. Still, there was no other choice.

She thought of the message she'd received weeks ago:

> *to ren, sign: #652382xa*
>
> *mountains impassable*
>
> *unable to assist, apologies*
>
> *come to us if you can, loc. 936*
>
> *sufficient food and shelter*
>
> *ra, sign: #898255yf*
>
> *Ad Solem Semper*

She didn't fully understand – 'Ad Solem Semper,' an archaic phrase from a forgotten language. And who was Ra? But it was the only hope they had.

Janis stood in the hallway, eyes red and swollen. Yet there was a determination to the boy. Ren thrust a coat into his arms. "We must go," she said softly.

He slipped it on, saying nothing, and then began putting on his shoes.

Returning upstairs, Ren found May propped against her pillows, laboring for breath. The room smelled of sickness and sorrow. Ren placed a hand over May's thin one. "Is there anything I can do to ease your pain? To make it... stop?"

"Just take my boy," May murmured. "He's a handful but... worth everything."

Ren squeezed gently. "Yes." She hesitated, voice low. "Do you want to know how long you –?"

"No," May breathed. "I won't make it to spring, will I?"

Ren gave her a solemn look, silent.

"Save them," May implored, voice breaking. "Save the valley if you can – these people aren't perfect, but they deserve a chance."

She bowed her head, then descended, something burning at the corners of her eyes.

They slipped into the night, moving like phantoms among empty houses. Rain hammered the roofs, thunder resonated across the sky. By the time they reached the edge of the forest, Janis's boots were soaked, his breath ragged. Ren pointed toward the mountains' dark silhouettes, looming like watchful giants. A slim figure and a smaller one, hearts heavy with new grief, trudged away from the dying glow of windows. Step after step, they vanished into the storm, following a faint hope beyond the valley's prison.

Winter soon enveloped them. And though they trembled with cold and heartbreak, they pressed on, clinging to each other's presence as they walked toward the horizon, toward anything that might offer hope. Always, they would follow the sun.